Copyr

Amazon Self

This Book first published in Gre.... _...... by Amazon 2021
© Iain C.M. Gray 2021

Iain C.M. Gray asserts his moral right to be identified as the author
of this work

The Ruined Road – Plus One

A Collection of Short Stories

By Iain C.M. Gray

Information about the author and details of other work by Iain C.M. Gray can be found at iaincmgray.com

Table of Contents

The Ruined Road

Story 1 - Anguish

The price of unchecked political ambition will always be human suffering.

On the morning of August the 20th in 1968 a sprightly Earnest Kozar ambled happily through V Botanice plaza on the way back to his apartment. Earnest had recently moved into this basic but cosy loft apartment with his newly wedded bride Renata. Their apartment block was situated on the corner of V Botanice and Preslova. Renata's mother and father had generously gifted them this fully furnished apartment to ensure Renata remained in an area that suited her social standing. Living in the Malá Strana district of Prague was, they thought, eminently appropriate for their beloved daughter.

Earnest had lived in Prague all his life. He came from a modest but hard-working family. By dint of dogged persistence and a sharp intellect Earnest had risen from his somewhat modest roots to study at Prague's prestigious University of Economics. It was there he met, and fell in love, with Renata.

Like many other Praguers, Earnest and Renata had been caught up in a surge of optimism that their country was now embracing the policies of ever-expanding freedom. Renata's parents, the Berezina's, and their associated social club members believed themselves to be key players in the ongoing battle for greater democratic rights. Through protest and persuasive arguments the Berezina's and their ilk believed the tide of change had become an inevitable, unstoppable, force. Renata's father considered the Mayor of Prague, Ludvik Chovanec, to be a close personal friend, though he also considered Mr Chovanec to be somewhat naive and foolish.

After buying the daily newspaper, chléb, and the latest copy of the Literární Listy, Earnest was returning to his apartment for breakfast, then he would leave to go to work as usual. The streets were quiet, but it was still early, so perhaps this was nothing to be particularly worried about. The atmosphere in Prague had recently soured somewhat, from being hopeful of a new dawn, to becoming increasingly fear fuelled and paranoic. Rumour upon rumour were being bandied about in markets, shops, and public houses, regarding a boiling Soviet backlash to the progressive ideas being implemented by Alexander Dubček. For young Earnest, recently married, good job, a nice new house in a well to do area, he steadfastly refused to have his hope dented by inveterate doom and gloom mongers.

After skipping up the stairs two at a time it was with great pride that Earnest drove his key into the front door of his new home. "I'm back," he announced loudly as he strode into the living room. He was greeted by the tinkling noise of teacups and the warm burbling of a kettle boiling.

A modest repast of cheese and jams had been set out atop a pristine white tablecloth, on the table by the window. An empty plate for the chléb took pride of place in the centre of the table. Earnest put the Literární Listy by Renata's plate and sat by his own to peruse his newspaper. He had no expectations that there would be anything of note, or indeed true, contained in the pages, but sometimes you could read between the lines and glean a fragment of an idea about what exactly was going on in his country. Censorship had recently been repealed, though public opinion was still to be swayed regarding the reliability of the news.

Coming backwards out the kitchen carrying a tray with a pot of tea, jug of cream and a pair of mugs, Renata smiled at her husband as she laid the tea tray on the table, "Ready for breakfast my love?"

Marvelling once again at the ethereal beauty of his wife Earnest laid down his paper and stood up, "I'm ready for breakfast, and some love my dear," he said as he held his wife tight and planted a playful kiss on her lips. Earnest regularly questioned the tangibility of his good fortune. He couldn't believe his luck.

Renata laughed, blushed ever so slightly, and playfully pushed him away, "Less of your nonsense Mr Kozar, we don't want you being late for work now do we?"

"Indeed Mrs Kozar, the wheels of industry would most certainly crumble to nought without my timely presence." Earnest worked as a junior surveyor.

In the silence that descended as they consumed their breakfast the Kozars became acutely aware of a distant rumbling sound approaching. With every passing second the incongruous noise grew in intensity; until their anxious curiosity could no longer be suppressed. They shot to standing to stare out their window in order to locate the source of such an ominous noise.

Incredibly, travelling at speed down V Botanice, with an armoured jeep in the lead, rolled a full battalion of Soviet tanks. Every tank was covered with a tight knit nest of heavily armed Soviet soldiers, stuck to the top like limpets. The unstoppable force of a communist dictatorship had descended on the immovable Prague like a prurient plague.

Praguers were pouring out of their houses on V Botanice to stand in the slip stream of the tanks. They gawped at the invading army, their faces etched with shock and painted puce with horror. Red, white, and blue Czech flags were brought out to be draped from various windows and slung over the shoulders of stoic Praguers as they watched with simmering anger while their country was invaded by the mighty Soviet army. The Soviets, so far, were being met only with passive, powerless, resistance, laced with incredulous, righteous, rage.

Earnest felt a chill of fear flow through his veins, it pooled in the pit of his stomach, he felt sick, the colour drained from his face leaving it as white as the tablecloth. "I can't believe they have actually done this," he just managed to say.

"Bastards," Renata hissed, angry fire projected from her icy blue eyes.

Their phone started ringing. Renata knew who it would be. She shot into the hall to speak with her mother.

Earnest watched the bored, restless looking soldiers getting ferried further into the city, as his mind tried to process what exactly this would mean for him, his new bride, and his new life. He listened to the half of the conversation he could hear Renata having with her mother.

"I know…….. I know………. Bastards……….. There are hundreds of them here……….. Where………….. When………….. I'll be there…………. I love you mother."

Renata hung up and came to stand beside her husband, she slipped her arm around his waist. "Mother and father are going to the town hall to protest." They watched the soldiers in silence, Earnest knew what was coming next, and he desperately wished it away. "I'm going to go with them," Renata added softly. The fear that had earlier gathered in the pit of his stomach shot out lightning bolts of premonitionary anxiety into his every fibre. Earnest knew in his heart that it would be futile to even attempt to counter her decision. Renata's indomitable spirit was one of the main reasons Earnest was attracted to her in the first place.

Earnest turned to face his wife, brushing back the hair from her eyes, he looked deep into her eyes, "Make sure you stay safe Renata." Earnest held her tight, "I think I'm going to have to go to work." Earnest had seen besuited office workers, carrying briefcases, strolling self-consciously alongside the advancing army. They had obviously decided to go to work as normal. Perhaps carrying on regardless, adopting a business-as-usual attitude, was also a way to register your refusal to accept this most extreme of impositions.

Blankly Earnest stared at the ordinary breakfast laid out on the table, then at the foreign soldiers pouring into his city and his life. His appetite had been instantly quashed.

Solemnly Earnest dressed in his best suit and overcoat. Renata remained fixated at the window staring with simmering rage at the sight of her city being raped by the Soviet army.

"I love you," Earnest stood, dressed for work, directly behind her. She turned and with tears in their eyes they held each other tightly.

"I love you too," Renata shouted as the front door shut firmly behind him.

Earnest stood on the street scanning the faces of the bored looking invaders as they rumbled past atop their tanks. The soldiers were being watched by the whole of Prague. They were assaulted only by the occasional volley of abuse delivered from the relative safety of various balconies. Darting between a gap in the tanks Earnest ran to the other side of the street to wave farewell to Renata, who was still standing, raging, at the window. Earnest tore himself away from the vision of his wife and rounded the corner to follow the tanks across the Vltava down into the old town.

Angry encounters, and fear-fuelled aggression accompanied Earnest on his journey into work. The incredulous natives were venting their collective spleens at the Soviets. To get to his office Earnest had to traverse the old town square. The normally active square had been taken over by the Red Army. Praguers were arguing openly with the Soviets demanding to know why they were here; the Soviets were countering with reminders about how welcome they were when they were liberating the country from the Nazi's in 1945. Earnest had to circumvent the square to get to his office.

In the office there were a couple of older workers nervously faking work-related activity. The younger employees were crowded round the small windows swapping stories about what they had seen on their way into work. They peered avidly at the various contretemps occurring on the square. There were reports swirling around the office about casualties, and pockets of resistance. The Mayor of Prague, Ludvik Chovanec, was reputed to be pounding the streets around the town hall pleading with Praguers and protestors that this was all normal and nothing to worry about, and that everything would still turn out for the good in the end.

Earnest sat at his desk and pulled out some documents from the side drawer, he flicked open some random draughting plans and started to pour over the pages. His seeming absorption in work prevented his colleagues from engaging with him and allowed his mind to retreat into thinking about what he should, or indeed could, do about this horrendous situation. His mind was permitted to roam unimpeded until:

BOOOOOOOOOOOOOM.

The old office windowpanes rattled as a nearby explosion reverberated around the old town. All pretences of work ceased immediately. Information about what had happened was not about to float into the office by osmosis, so all the staff grabbed their coats and ran out into the streets. An explosion simply had to be investigated, Earnest, of course, went with them.

A bus on Křižovnická has been set alight and had exploded. Whether it was Soviet or Czech that had set the bus on fire was unknown. Whether or not these were any dead or injured was also unknown. Sporadic gunfire could now be heard resounding around the city from various points. In the streets of the old town, the auditory proof of intensified violence only exacerbated the already taught, angry, tension.

Earnest knew where Renata would be, so he went directly there, his coat tails flapping behind him as he ran.

As he approached the town hall square Earnest could hear the angry shouts of protestors. "Get out our country NOW," they chanted over and over.

Standing on the tips of his toes Earnest searched frantically over the heads of the Soviet soldiers who had surrounded a small group of protestors marching up and down outside the town hall. Being surrounded by soldiers pointing semi-automatic weapons at them had not quelled their anger or silenced their voice in any way shape or form.

Renata was there. Standing in the front row of the protestors, with her parents beside her, her face was twisted with rage as she railed against the foreign intruders. Earnest felt ashamed that he had not accompanied her earlier. His previous attitude of stoicism, and commitment to his work now felt to him more like bare faced cowardice.

Earnest shouted to her, but his lone voice was drowned out in the swamp of noise rollicking around the square. Agitated he waved his arms about and bobbed up and down desperately trying to get her attention.

A small nearby explosion caused one of the soldier's already frayed nerves to snap. He unleashed a split-second volley of machine gun fire directly into the protestors. Earnest watched on in horror as his wife took a bullet directly to her chest. It knocked her back and down. She fell along with a few of her fellow protestors, including her mother and father.

"Noooooo," Earnest howled as he elbowed past the line of soldiers to sprint to his fallen wife, her body was limp and lifeless as he picked her up to hold her close to his chest, her blood pumped out and spewed over his clothes. Renata had died, instantly.

Earnest howled at the sky, and this time his voice was heard. An eery silence descended on the square as the reality of what had happened rammed itself home to all involved. The soldiers primed themselves and were fully prepared to fight if the reaction of the remaining protestors was violent. They needn't have worried, the reaction of the protestors was shock, horror, and searing fear. The prospect of death was now very real and personal.

Looking up with tears streaming down his blood-smeared face, Earnest looked into the wide eyes of Ludvik Chovanec, the Mayor of Prague. Stunned, Ludvik tried to splutter the rubbish he had been spouting all day, about how everything will still be all-right, that people just needed to hang on and not do anything silly.

"How," Earnest screamed at him. "How is everything going to be all-right." Earnest stood up, cradling his wife's dead body in his arms. "My wife is dead you blind idiot. Things are never going to be all-right." Earnest pushed past the mayor and forced his way through the cordon of soldiers. Most of the soldiers looked just as shocked as the protestors. The soldiers melted back, and Earnest was met with no resistance as he left the square carrying his dead wife.

Ashen faced, Earnest trod slowly through the streets of Prague cradling the empty shell of his Renata. No one looked at him, they were afraid of his pain; and he looked at no one, he had interest in nothing. The sounds of the streets seemed to filter through marshmallows rammed in his ears. He heard only muffled white noise.

Earnest had just had his future brutally ripped from him, and his present was only searing, unendurable, pain. He decided to do the only thing he could possibly think to do. With his decision made a peaceful calm descended in his breast and flowed out to his extremities. His mind was numb, cold, and calm.

As he carried his wife's body through the chaotic streets of his city he felt her cool as the warmth of her life dissipated. Renata's life blood emptied, and soon they stopped leaving a gory trail behind them. Earnest's clothes were plastered with her coagulating blood.

Reaching their home Earnest tramped slowly up the stairs he had leapt up only a few hours ago. This now seemed like an impossible lifetime away. Placing Renata gently on the sofa Earnest searched the hall cupboard for the jerry can of petrol he knew was there.

Carrying the can in one hand, and cradling the body of Renata in his arms, Earnest left his home. He didn't bother closing the door, he knew he wasn't going to be returning.

No one noticed him as he tramped deliberately down to the banks of the Vltava to deposit his wife's corpse in the river. Tears welled in his eyes and spilled down his cheeks, ploughing their way through dried blood as he finally kissed his wife goodbye. Earnest watched as the tide carried the body of his dead soulmate away downstream, her long hair rolling and flowing in the waves.

Rage surged through his body as he picked up the jerry can of petrol. Earnest marched away from the river and up onto the Charles bridge. Restless soldiers meandered aimlessly this way and that. Praguers scurried over the bridge, some shouting their impotent anger, some crying out their fears, some rushing quickly to check on the safety of loved ones.

Earnest stood in the middle of the bridge and poured the entire contents of the jerry can over his head. He was drenched in petrol. Fixing a stare on an approaching soldier Earnest pulled a cigarette lighter out his pocket. The soldier sensed the horror about to be enacted out in front of his eyes. The poor soldier tried to tear his gaze away from Earnest's raging glare, but he was transfixed by the angry young man's ferocious glower. "THIS IS ON YOU, YOU BASTARD," Earnest yelled at the soldier; spit and petrol spraying from his mouth. Earnest held up his arm and rolled the wheel of the lighter, white sparks flew. Flames sped down his arm and Earnest was swallowed up in a massive fireball of surely fatal flames.

Story 2 - Liberation

"Candy, would you just fucking shift your lazy ass and get the fuck out there. You're missing the golden hour."

"All right, all right. I'm nearly ready, I just gotta get my face on properly."

"You're beautiful, Cand. You look like a million dollars already. They won't be able to resist you."

I can't believe this fucking guy. He thinks he knows everything. Let's see him be all, "You're beautiful my love," *if I end up coming back here with nothing. He is just so full of shit. The more of this crap I put on my face, the more the punters like it, the faster I can make my money and be done. I just need a little bit more lippy and I'm ready for yet another night. What did Bette Davis say?* 'Men become much more attractive when they start looking older. But it doesn't do much for women, though we do have an advantage: make-up'. *I wonder what she would have made of Rudy, he's certainly NOT gotten more attractive. Oh well, here goes another night, same as the last, and the last before that, and every fucking night for the last two years.*

"Candy, for fuck's sake. If you don't get out of this fucking house now I'm gonna put my boot through your fucking ass, and kick you out of the fucking door without opening it. Ok?"

"Sorry Rudy love, sorry. I'm going. I'm going." *Keep your fucking hair on little man, you don't have much hair left to lose, bald fucking idiot.*

"I'll pop round Belle's in a couple of hours Cand. See how you're getting on eh? I sure could use another bottle of Jack."

"Sure thing Rude. See you in a couple of hours at Belle's sweetheart."

"Bye."

God it's cold tonight. Happy fucking Christmas. And I can't even wear a jacket. These fuckers drive up in their nice warm cars, with their thick coats, and still they expect you to be wearing next to nothing. Is it the time that it takes to get my coat off? Is that it? Can they not wait a second longer for me to take off a fucking coat? Or is it that they like to see us miserable and cold? Do they hate us that much? Or do they not even consider us for long enough to hate us. They just don't fucking care is probably what it comes down to. Bastards. Well, as long as I get my money, what do I care. D Street here I come, again.

"What's up sugar? How you doing?"

Same place, same people, saying the same things, over and over, again and again. What happened to all the promises of a bunch of kids and a nice house with a picket fence and a garden? "Hey Dee Dee. How's it going? You turned any tricks yet? How's traffic tonight?"

"Been out here nearly two fuckin' hours and all I've had was a lousy fucking blow-job round the back of McDonalds."

I'm not surprised, you can smell her from here, even against the wind. The older they get the less they care about looking after themselves. As soon as personal hygiene goes out the window it's time to hang up the bra. "Things will pick up sugar. It's golden hour now. Looks like the traffic is picking up."

"No one stopping though Cand. You think the Five O are out again tonight?"

"Nah. Too cold Dee Dee. They'll all be in the jailhouse drinking coffee and eating doughnuts. Fat bastards." *They'll be out later though, for their cut. Rudy first, then the cops, then Belle. They are all lining up to get their cut. I do all the work and they take all the money. I suppose that's just the way it is. The way it's always been. The way it always will be.* "You been up to Belle's tonight Dee?"

"Fuck no. That bitch just keeps rousting me up for money she says I owe. I don't owe that cow jack shit Cand. I swear. I think she's got it in for me."

My heart bleeds. It's probably cause every time you are up there you stink out the toilets and do nothing else but moan about shit. "She's just funny sometimes Dee. You know what she's like."

"I like your hair like that by the way. I been thinking 'bout going blonde myself. You think it would suit me?"

"Yeah, Dee, it would match your skin perfectly." *Sad cow, nothing is going to change her looks, or her luck. She just needs to go work in a diner or something. It's gotta be better than dishing out blow jobs at the back of McDonalds for a five.*

God this town is nothing but a shit hole.

"You got a smoke Cand?"

"Sure, here."

"You got a light?"

Do you want me to smoke the fucking thing for you? "You seen Simone yet?"

"Nah, she'll be working out of Belle's. Street's too cold for that lazy bitch in December."

Would love to see her call Simone a lazy bitch to her face. She'd rip her face off. Smile Candy doll, smile, there's some action coming.

"Hey ladies. How you all doing? Hey blondie, you looking hot tonight!"

Is he fucking joking? I'm freezing my fucking tits off. "Hey sugar, I'm hot for you alright. You wanna go have some fun?"

"That's my middle name sweetheart, I'm always up for a bit of fun. You got somewhere we can go?"

"You just follow me sugar."

"What's your name sweetheart?"

"Candy."

"Pleased to meet you Candy. I'm John."

Yeah sure, another fucking John. Say hi to your wife from me eh John. "Very pleased to meet you too John. Let's go Belle's so we can get to know each other better eh?"

I suppose he looks harmless enough. You never can tell though. I thought that son of a bitch Rudy looked harmless enough and look what happened there? Then there was that hillbilly asshole that tried it on with Simone. He sure picked the wrong one there to try it on with. Never seen such a sight as him jumping down the steps at Belle's with his pants round his ankles.

"Are you laughing at me?"

"Oh sorry, John, I was just thinking 'bout something funny I watched on TV earlier. Here we are sugar. I'll just sort us out a room."

Nice one, I'm glad she's here, "Hi Simone. Dee Dee said you'd be here. You seen Belle? I need a room?" *Simone looks different tonight. No make-up? What's going on with her? Is she not working? How?*

"Hey sugar. Belle's out the back. Most of the rooms is free. Take your pick, it's a slow night. Reckon Suze is in 6. Other than that the choice is yours."

"Hi John."

"How did you know my name?"

"Lucky guess I suppose. You give me a shout if you need Cand?"

"Will do Simone. Let's go have us some fun John eh?" *As much fun as getting slapped in the face with a wet fish. Suze is a screamer, so I reckon I'll stay down this end. 1's as good as any I suppose.*

"Let's get the messy business out the way first John. Cash up front!" *After I dole out to all of them freeloaders I'll have nothing left. Wonder if I can avoid the cops tonight?* "Thanks John. I just got to go powder my nose. You get yourself comfortable sweetheart. I'll be back in a tic."

God, I'm starting to look old. Just got to put a little bit of this.........in there........ Hair is looking good. That prick better not mess it up. Now I'm ready.

"Mmmmm, John, you did indeed get yourself comfortable. I'm ready too my love. I am so hot for you John." *What the fuck! Has he been hard all this time? He must have been playing with himself, dirty bastard. At least he's not totally ugly. And he doesn't seem to smell bad.*

"No kissing John. I just washed my hair."

There goes Suze. Boy she has got some set of lungs on her. I swear she just does it to freak them out.

I wish 'John' would just hurry up and get it over with, I'm dying for a smoke. By the looks of things he's not gonna take long. He fucks like a jackhammer.

I must remember to get some eggs on the way home, I'm in the mood for pancakes.

"Oh, John, I'm gonna cum."

Probably best get bacon too.

"Mmmmm, you got a smoke John? That was GOOD honey. Thanks. I just gotta go freshen up now sugar, be back in 5."

Well at least I've earned something already. Could do with at least one more punter before Rudy pitches up, or I reckon I'll be in trouble. I think I'm getting wrinkles, and my chin is sinking. Wonder how long I have left before I end up like Dee Dee? Was that the door?

"John?" *Fucking hell. Bastard didn't even wait to say goodbye.*

"You ok up there Candy?"

"I'm fine Simone. Another one that doesn't even have the common decency to say goodbye. What the fuck ever happened to all the decent men round here?"

"In San Bernadino? Are you fucking kidding me? They all went long time ago. If there ever were any. Come and have a drink with me Candy. I got something I wanna talk to you about."

Better remember to go pay Belle, "What's up Simone? You turned any tricks tonight?"

"Here, have a Scotch Cand, you've earned it. No tricks for me tonight Candy, and if things work out like I want, there's going to be no more tricks for me ever. That's what I wanted to talk to you about. You could chuck this miserable existence as well if you wanted to."

I really don't get why everybody drinks this stuff, it's horrible. No more tricks? Sounds like heaven.

Never heard Simone talk like that though. Wonder what she's got going on?

"Thing is Candy. I've met someone."

Ah here it comes. 'He's going to save me. He really loves me.' *How could someone like Simone fall for that old crap?*

"Now I know what you're thinking. But it's not like that Candy. He's a priest."

Fuck, Simone, we've all fucked a preacher. They're no different, they're just more deluded.

"He's different. He's not after me for my body, he's not even after my soul. What he wants is to set up an outreach service for the girls. He's not wanting to convert anybody; he just wants to help us 'troubled' people. Said it was something to do with Mary Magdalene or something. He's got money from the church and he's going to get a bus, somewhere the girls can go escape the streets for a bit, get something to eat and free condoms. And I'll be there to talk to them. You too if you want to, you know? You can give them a shoulder to cry on when they need it."

Is she for real? What the fuck is his angle? "So you giving up the streets?"

"I'm sick of it Candy. But there's no way I could just go work in a bar or something. I'd end up back on my back before the first shift was over."

"So what you going to do for money? How you going to pay your rent?"

"I got a bit tucked by for a rainy-day Candy. And I've looked into it, I can register as a charity and get local businesses to donate. They get tax breaks if they donate to charity. And the priest is going to get us hand outs and stuff for the girls, the church gets loads of stuff. I got a few businesses interested already. Cand, thing is, I can't do it on my own. I want you to do it with me. You can come stay at mine. You know you need to get yourself away from that fuck-wit Rudy. Right?"

She's lost the plot. I mean yes I need to get out of this life and away from Rudy, but this is mad. I mean who is this priest anyway. "Wow, sugar, I gotta think a bit about that. You're talking some big stuff Simone."

I gotta get out of here before I catch her loony. "BELLE. I'M LEAVING YOUR RENT IN THE VASE."

"I need to hit the streets again Simone. I'll catch you later about, you know, your idea 'n'all."

"I know Cand. It's big stuff for me too. But what's there to think about? We deserve better than this Candy. Think about it when you're on your back with another one of them fuckers bouncing about on top of you, drooling on your face."
But how is 'donations' gonna match what I make in a night on the streets? It's not even gonna get close. "See you laters Simone."

Fuck it is cold tonight. Dee Dee must be back round the back of McDonalds. Oh no, not tonight please, not tonight, "Evening officers. What are you guys doing out on a cold night like this?"

"We was just gonna ask you the same thing Candy. And without a coat as well. What do we think of that Lou?"

"I'd say it was a fucking dumb ass thing to do Randy. Is what I would say. And I don't much like dumb asses."

There is no-one round here that's a dumber ass than you two, "Awww don't be like that officers, I'm just a poor girl who lost her jacket is all."

"We're collecting for the poor again tonight Candy. Would you like to contribute? And when I say would you like to contribute what I really mean is give us a twenty or your busted. Ok?"

Fuck, fuck, fuck, after Rudy has his cut I'm gonna be left with nothing, "C'mon officers, give a girl a break eh? I ain't even got a twenty."

"Be a night in the cells for you then."

"Ok, ok, ok, here," *I can't believe this. I need another John, and quick.*

"And you can fuck off from the streets for tonight 'n'all Candy. You're making our town look dirty."

Fucking bastards. So I gotta go back to Belle's and listen to her droning on about her mad fucking priest. Fuck. "Fucking pigs."

"What did you say?"

"Nothing officers. I said have a nice day."

"You just better keep walking bitch. And best just run the next time you see us coming."

I suppose any 'donations' would be better than what I've got right now. And that's my night over now; if they see me out again I'm busted for sure.

"Hey Simone, cops are out tonight, got their pound of flesh out of me." *Could I just chuck it? Outreach service for the girls? Some of them are pitiful, they sure could use a good feed and some help. And the young girls that are pitching up these days? They could sure use a wise head to keep them right.*

"It's never going to change Candy. It's the way it's always been, and the way it always will be. You know that right?"

"What we gonna do about them bastards? Cops won't take too kindly to us pitching up in a bus feeding the girls and doling out condoms?"

"Chief of Police is an old client of mine. I do a bit of leaning, mention his wife's name a few times to him, he'll make sure we're left alone."

"You've thought of everything you ain't ya."

"You know me Candy. I cover all my bases. Here comes trouble. If he lays a hand on you he is fucking history Candy."

"Hey Candy, you here?"

"In here Rudy. I'm just sitting with Simone."

"You got anything yet? I need another bottle."

"You look like you've had enough already."

"You mind your own business; I wasn't talking to you. Cand? You got any money?"

"All I got is this Rude. I swear this is all I got. The fucking cops were up my ass just now. They fleeced me."

"Are you fucking kidding? That's not even enough for a bottle of Jack! Do you want me to have to drink that gut-rot? Fucking give it here anyways. You going back out?"

He's gonna blow, I can see it in his eyes. "I can't Rudy love, the cops will haul my ass in jail if I go back out."

"What do you think I'm gonna fucking do to you if you don't.........? What kind of pussy do you think I am..........? YOU JUST SHIFT YOUR FUCKING FAT ASS BACK OUT THERE AND GET ME MY BOTTLE."

"You're not welcome here Rudy. You need to leave."

"I already tole you to mind your own fucking business."

"Little man. It is time for you to leave. I won't tell you again."

"You don't get to tell me anything. What the fuck? Owwww. Owwww. Owwww. Leave me alone. Owwww. Let go my fucking arm you fucking bitch."

"Just taking the rubbish out Candy. I'll be back in a mo."

Absolutely nobody messes with Simone. You know what? If there's anybody can make this outreach thing work, it's her. "Where did you learn to do all that stuff Simone?"

"Self-defence classes. Something else we can teach the girls on our bus. You up for it Cand?"

Candy still wasn't completely convinced, but she knew Simone was right, and that the only way things were going to end up if she did nothing, was badly. Candy cracked a weary smile at Simone, "Fuck it Simone, let's do it."

Story 3 - Fear

The two moons of Lunesta rose resplendent, looking like a luminescent infinity symbol floating heavily in the sky. Heavy, pink, methane clouds rolled over the bare hills that overlooked Serendipity city, the capital, and sole city, of this small, hostile, planet.

Castor Stark strode through the main thoroughfare of new town district, with his entourage trailing in his wake. Castor stopped to stare at the sky, "The asteroid showers are getting worse. If we don't do something, and do it now, we face certain destruction." His entourage mumbled and groaned in gloomy agreement.

In anticipation of an oncoming shower the oxidising squad were out preparing to treat the methane rain once it fell. As Castor marched past they stopped their activities and bowed formally to honour their leader.

"And that wayward brother of mine," continued Castor, "And his deluded followers, will no doubt be completely ignoring the current catalogue of ill omens," Castor voiced his exasperation to Folas Adliz, his chief advisor.

"We can explore all available options tonight when the council committee is convened sire," Folas replied making a note in his note pad, though increasingly there was only ever one main topic of discussion at council meetings - what to do about the increasingly reckless activities of Castor's brother, Azuca Stark, and his expanding gang of hedonistic heathens. Azuca and his followers steadfastly refused to conform to conventional wisdom regarding the precarious future of life on Lunesta.

"Science has a solution for everything; but it has so far failed to cure the troubling condition of wanton indulgence," Castor observed as he and his entourage marched into and through the foyer of Serendipity council city hall.

"Folas, my chambers, ten minutes. I want a full briefing on tonight's assembly." Castor waved away his entourage.

"Yes sire," Folas respectfully bowed his way backwards and away from his leader as he headed for his office.

Castor climbed the austere staircase that rose from the middle of the ground floor lobby, over the council chambers, to his modest second floor office. On the third floor there were smaller offices, housing other lower rank assembly members, and smaller meeting rooms. In the large basement there was a shared eating space and more offices that housed the facility management staff.

Standing at the large window in his office, Castor stared out at the small brick structures that made up Serendipity city. Most of the dwellings were only one floor high, though there were a couple of other council buildings that rose higher. The council ran everything that ensured the smooth running of Serendipity city: food production, scientific research, policing, and infrastructure development and maintenance. Due to extreme climactic conditions all the buildings had large basement rooms and most of the living quarters were located underground.

Existence had been hard fought for on Lunesta. The resident population had survived by persisting with the cultivation of the small numbers of edible plants and mosses that had managed to survive on this hostile planet. Lunestrans had evolved physically and had the ability to convert even the smallest amount of nourishment into energy, which they then stored in every cell of their physical form to utilise when required. Life was treated with the greatest respect, and anything that caused a risk to life was abolished, banned, or irradicated by their advanced scientific measures. Azuca Stark grew up challenging these ideas and philosophies. Azuca Stark had dedicated his life to not just survival but to seeking and indulging in every pleasure imaginable.

Dwelling on dark thoughts that disturbed his serenity Castor became aware of an insistent knocking on his office door. Blinking away the distance he had travelled from his here and now, Castor brought himself back to the present. "Come," he instructed the source of the knocking.

Bowing deeply Folas entered Castors office, "Sire, I have the briefings for this evenings business."

"How much of it relates to my brother Folas?"

"Most of the items, either directly or indirectly. It appears Azuca and his followers have managed to distil a new substance from one of the plants we have been cultivating. This substance causes, 'pleasurable sensations' to be experienced by the person imbibing it. I believe it is called Mochial sire."

In silence Castor rubbed his throbbing temples with one hand as the pain caused by Folas's report rattled through his mind. Castor sighed heavily, "And no doubt there will be the usual dearth of solutions from council assembly."

"Unfortunately, it's unlikely there will be any new ideas from anyone sire." Folas ensured his facial expression conveyed nothing but impartiality.

"Folas. This conversation goes no further than this office ok?" Castor's eyes pled a vulnerability that cracked Folas's fixed facade, and an expression of surprise momentarily crossed his normally unresponsive face.

"Of course sire. May I sit down?"

"Of course Folas," Castor remained standing in front of the window but gestured for Folas to avail himself of a seat on the other side of his desk.

With his hands clasped behind his back Castor strode up and down behind his desk, "What would happen to his followers if Azuca was removed, Folas?"

"What do you mean removed sire?"

"I mean, eliminated." Castor stopped walking and stared directly into Folas's eyes. "Let me speak plainly Folas. I mean killed. What would happen to his movement if my brother were killed?"

Survival had been so hard fought for on Lunesta that life had always been considered sacrosanct. There had never been a murder on Lunesta. What Castor Stark was proposing was so extreme and radical that Folas struggled to respond. "I, I, I," Folas stammered, "I suppose his movement would crumble. But no one would be able to do it sire. We are not capable."

Castor returned to stare out of the window at his city, "Perhaps I am though Folas. Perhaps I need to be." Castor returned to the darkness pervading his soul.

Meanwhile far away in another part of town, on the outskirts of Serendipity city, Azuca Stark strolled down a narrow road with his friend Lowsu. Azuca stared in wonder at the bright flashes of the asteroids as they peppered the sky with their sparkling trails.

"So beautiful Lowsu, I often wonder what else is out there," Azuca tried to stare beyond the brightness cast by Lunesta's two moons.

Lowsu was a childhood friend of both Castor and Azuca, though as Castor grew up, and ascended the ranks of power, he had put some distance between himself and his childhood acquaintances.

"Are you going to try some Mochial again tonight Lowsu?"

"I've tried it already Azuca. I didn't like it. It made me feel funny."

"It's supposed to make you feel funny Lowsu. That's the whole point."

"Castor wouldn't like you doing it. And he wouldn't like you telling others to do it too."

"To blazes with Castor and his cronies. They have been telling us what to do for years. It's time we lived a little Lowsu. It's time we explored the world within and the world without." Azuca twirled around the street with his arms thrown wide, "This is the era of discovery Lowsu. Instead of just striving to survive, it's time we flew and thrived."

Lowsu didn't really understand how sitting about drinking Mochial and talking about strange things constituted thriving, but he didn't share this thought with Azuca.

"I think we should all leave this drab city Lowsu. We should all go set ourselves up in one of the smaller colonies as far away from this dull hole as possible."

"Have you ever been out of Serendipity city Azuca?" Lowsu knew the answer, but he wanted to make Azuca think about the reality of what life was really like outside of the city. Lowsu knew what life was like in the colonies. It was hard work, and premature death was the most likely outcome for anyone living there.

"I hope you're not being your usual dreary self Lowsu. That's why you need to take more Mochial my friend."

Lowsu and Azuca entered a small dwelling to be greeted with a warm rousing welcome. A Mochial party was well under way. Azuca was greeted with great enthusiasm. Lowsu stayed long enough so as not appear rude, then he quietly removed himself to sit outside on a large rock where he could gaze at the colourful skies.

Meanwhile in city hall Castor descended the stairway that led directly from his office straight into the council assembly room. Folas followed at a respectful distance. The twelve senior councillors were in situ as protocol dictated. As one they stopped their discoursing, and stood silently as their leader entered the chambers.

Castor sat with Folas at his side and indicated that council business should proceed. Folas read out agenda items one after the other. These issues were debated at length, with Castor issuing orders, after demonstrating careful consideration of the issues discussed. Castor had no desire for proceedings to continue for any longer than they had to, but he carefully observed expected propriety. Azuca and his followers were discussed in detail throughout, small legislative changes were demanded and were uniformly passed.

As Folas formally brought meeting to an end Castor and the councillors rose, Castor nodded his head and his councillors bowed deeply. Folas followed Castor back up into his office as the twelve councillors solemnly left the chamber.

Castor sat at his desk, Folas sat opposite, "Sire, if I may be so bold as to broach the somewhat sensitive subject mentioned earlier."

"Please, speak freely Folas. I'm sure you will not be saying anything I have not considered one hundred times over."

"Azuca, and his followers," Folas paused, forming the words as perfectly as he could, "Surely this nonsense of theirs will just burn itself out naturally sire. Surely they will all come to their senses and realise that the only sensible thing to do would be to return to a life of working for the common good? I am sure if they are given long enough they will understand the need for the utmost safety in all our undertakings. They will come to understand that we need demonstrable prudence from all, including themselves."

Castor clasped his hands and held them against his pursed lips, "Folas, no one knows my brother better than I. His obsession will know no bounds, his dedication to dereliction will only increase exponentially. His infectious madness will only pull in as many peripheral people surrounding him as possible. He will be nought but an out-of-control tornado until some external force is brought to bear on his being."

"And you are that external force sire?" Tears came to Folas's eyes as he uttered what would previously have been an unthinkable concept.

The stoical strength emanating from his leader left him in no doubt as to the answer, "I'm coming with you then sire." Folas rose and bustled about re-arranging his cloak and dusting himself down, eager to demonstrate his readiness to accompany his leader wherever he should prescribe.

"As you wish Folas. You have always been a loyal advisor, and I would expect nothing less from you." Castor was impatient to do what had to be done while the winds of courage blew in his sails. "You must know that this will likely be a most unpleasant task. But I have considered all possibilities and I believe we are left with no other options. This simply has to be done. Tonight will be an infamous but historic night Folas."

Folas bowed his head, and followed Castor out of his office and out of city hall onto the streets of Serendipity City.

Lowsu sat on his rock listening to the sounds of merry making coming from the dwellings behind him. Somewhat detached he noted the disgust writ large on the faces of passers-by as they returned home from work. Lowsu thought about Castor and Azuca and about how he missed spending time with them both. Lowsu missed Castor's strength and solidity. Lowsu was also concerned about Azuca who was demonstrably spiralling inevitably downwards into ever greater depravity.

Lowsu was extremely surprised to see Castor Stark striding down the street towards him, with his chief advisor by his side. Lowsu stood and bowed his head to greet them.

Castor smiled, seeing his childhood friend on this inauspicious evening pleased him, "Lowsu, old friend, how are you?"

"I am well my leader. And all the happier for seeing you, though the pleasure is indeed unexpected," Lowsu was nervous, it had been a long time since he had spoken with Castor.

"Please Lowsu. We know each other too well for you not to call me by my given name."

Lowsu relaxed and smiled a broad smile, "So what brings you down here then Castor?"

Castor looked pointedly at the dwelling where incongruous noises sang out in the normally silent night, "I came to see my brother, Lowsu. Is he in there?"

Consternation crossed Lowsu's face and left behind a deep frown, "Yes, Azuca is in there I'm afraid."

"I'm glad you have not succumbed to the temptations encouraged by Azuca my friend. I think it not a good idea if I am seen to enter such a premises. Would you be so kind as to fetch my brother for me Lowsu? I urgently need to speak with him."

"I'll try Castor," Lowsu tentatively pushed his way through the door, he knew all too well the possible sights he would be met with.

For the first time in his life Folas knew not what to say, and Castor was in no mood to share his thoughts. So master and chief stood in silence contemplating the colours the asteroids caused as they passed over the wispy methane clouds.

Lowsu eventually returned, dragging an obviously intoxicated Azuca behind him. Lowsu presented Azuca to Castor, "I told you, your brother is here to speak with you Azuca. Please pay him some close attention Azuca." Lowsu and Folas respectfully backed away and left the two brothers facing each other, Castor stern and solid, Azuca fluid and swaying.

Castor's pent-up anger boiled up again, it stiffened his resolve, "You bring shame on our family Azuca. How can you let yourself get into such a state?"

Azuca battled to focus on his brother, "Castor, if you have only come to lecture me once again, you have wasted your time. And I am not in the slightest bit interested in you wasting any more of my precious time. Goodbye." Azuca turned to return to the party.

Castor grabbed his wrist, "No. Please Azuca. We need to talk about something of the utmost importance." Castor couldn't allow this chance to pass him by, he wasn't sure he would ever be able to summon the courage to commit the act that had been haunting his thoughts so obsessively again.

Azuca had never heard his brother begging with such vulnerability. It had a sobering effect on him, and he responded by yielding to Castor as he led him away. "Come with me up to Adeilnoost ridge Azuca. I have a proposal to put to you."

Adeilnoost ridge stood at the head of a deep gully that had previously been heavily quarried for stone to build Serendipity city.

As the four traipsed up the hill to the ridge Folas introduced himself to Lowsu and made polite conversation. Castor walked on distracted by his thoughts, he looked at every footfall he took, and saw nothing. Azuca babbled a virtually incoherent stream of words and loosely connected ideas that reached only deaf ears.

As they neared the ridge Folas strategically dropped further and further behind the two brothers, he made sure to keep Lowsu engaged and distracted. Castor and Azuca carried on to stand close to the edge of the ridge.

Castor had previously planned this moment in its every detail, but now the time had come his plan to throw Azuca over the ridge flew from his mind and he became riven with doubt. "Azuca, I'm begging you, please renounce this life of debauchery and foolishness. Come home with me and let us set our world straight on its true path."

Azuca stared incredulously at his brother, "You brought me all the way up here for this? What was all that about a proposal? Is that it?" Anger surged in Azusa's breast, "I told you Castor. DON'T WASTE MY TIME."

Azuca made to stride past his brother. Rage boiled over in Castor, and he acted on instinct, his hands gripped Azuca by the neck. Castor tripped Azuca and fell on top of him, his hands gripped Azuca's throat like a vice. Panic bled from Azuca's eyes as his hands sought to free his throat. His strength was no match for his brother's.

As Castor slayed Azuca a stunned Lowsu grappled to comprehend what was going on. Folas readied himself to intervene should Azuca's friend try to foil Castor's plan. He needn't have bothered, Lowsu was frozen still with dread.

As life ebbed out of Azuca, Castor sat back aghast. Horror pulsed violently through his system. This was not what he expected to feel. Castor envisaged experiencing heroic feelings of a honourable sacrificial mission being completed. All he did feel was sick and wracked with self-repulsion. As he looked into the dead eyes of his brother Castor's vision tunnelled vertiginously.

Castor stood and looked back at the horrified faces of Lowsu and Folas, "It wasn't supposed to be like this," Castor mumbled. "I can't.....................」 Castor didn't finish his sentence. He picked up the dead body of his brother and leapt silently off Adeilnoost ridge.

Lowsu turned to Folas, "What's going on?" he asked, incredulity imprinted on his every feature.

"I think our world has just changed forever," was all Folas managed to reply.

Story 4 - Abuse

Soberly dressed, in a charcoal grey pin stripe, the grey-haired balding bishop sprayed his gaze around the room, which was filled with eager, fervent, Mormons. The deacons were occupied dutifully distributing small portions of just blessed sacramental bread and water. Bright summer sunbeams shone through tiny windows sited high up on sparklingly clean, plain, whitewashed walls.

There were no baptisms or confirmations due, so, once the sacramental offerings were dispensed, the bishop duly announced the first speaker from the congregation to deliver a talk.

The Hansen family sat, the same as the rest of the congregation, backs straight, dressed in Sunday best, modest, clean, and neat. Ammon, the father, was scheduled to deliver the final talk of the service. Mild murmurs of approval rippled occasionally from the congregations as the talks, loaded with scripture, were delivered with suitably subdued sincerity.

"And now," the bishop announced, "Last, but by no means least, my good friend Ammon Hansen will round off this fine morning by reminding us about the importance of the sacrament."

With great humility and dignity Ammon took the stand, "Friends, I have lived alongside you for over 40 years now. I have lived happily in this good god-fearing town my whole life. I have watched it grow from the small farming community it was when I was born, to become the large, thriving, farming community it is now. My only wish now would be that my dear son and daughter get to stay here for their whole lives too, to watch our little town continue to grow and be filled with more friendly, wholesome, people like yourselves." Ammon's stony faced twitched in what, for him, passed for a smile.

Ammon's wife and son, Sariah, and Layton, smiled broadly at Ammon; they were appropriately proud and emotionally aligned with his message. Ammon's daughter, Olivia, distracted by conflicting thoughts, stared at her feet as they scuffled against each other fidgeting to fly free.

Ammon continued, "But without the good grace of God, and our continued dedication to understanding and following His word, our little town and our decent way of life will, most assuredly, be threatened from outside influences. As the good book says, 'And that thou mayest more fully keep thyself unspotted from the world, thou shalt go to the house of prayer and offer up thy sacraments upon my holy day. For verily this is a day appointed unto you to rest from your labours, and to pay thy devotions unto the Most High.' Worldly temptations are, I'm afraid, forever knocking on our doors friends. It is surely only by harnessing the strength of the lord that we can fully resist these moral abominations in order to continue to live our lives in good Christian order."

Ammon directed his talk to the congregation in general, but the more he talked the more Olivia's body language spoke of her deep discomfort with the words he spoke.

Ammon raised his voice as he started to become emotionally overcome with the power of the message he was delivering, "Amusement, laughter, light-mindedness, are all out of place in our most precious and essential sacrament meetings, as they are in our normal lives. We need to always assemble in the spirit of prayer, of meekness, with devotion in our hearts and we should all continue to live and breathe in this very way, every day, in every aspect of our lives." Ammon bowed his head; his talk was finished.

Muted mumbles of endorsement rumbled around the room as the sacrament, and Ammon's talk came to a satisfying close. Ammon returned to sit with his family. Sariah was glowing with pride, Layton was, as ever, awed by his father's solid presence, he was acutely aware of the respect others had for his father. Olivia wished for nothing more than to shrink and disappear. She was aware this wish would not come true, she shored up and reinforced her fragile internal dialogue regarding her own version of the truth about life in their town.

"I thank you all for coming here on this fine morning," beaming, the bishop rounded up the proceedings, "Let us pray in silence." Clasping his hands at his bowed face, the bishop led the congregation in silent prayer. "Let us now go and enjoy this good, God given day," flashing a substantial smile, the bishop brought the meeting to end.

A gentle hum filled the room as the congregation shared their thoughts about the service while they filed out the church. As she stepped into the bright sunlight the sun reflected off Olivia's pristine white dress, causing her to squint, "Mom, I'm going to go into town for a bit. Is that ok?", Olivia smiled at her mother.

Ammon rounded swiftly on Olivia, "Remember you have your Young Women's meeting tonight Olivia.

And we will need your help on the farm before that. And you need to help you mother prepare dinner tonight. Do you really think you have enough time to go gallivanting around town?" As he was speaking Ammon felt his anger rise.

Olivia adopted a contrite posture, "Father, I will of course attend to my duties, but first I need to attend to some school business in town. I shall be back in good time to perform my duties. I promise." Olivia smiled the sweetest most innocent smile for her father.

"Give her the benefit of the doubt Ammon," Sariah supported her daughter and sought to placate her husband. "You won't let us down again will you Olivia?"

A penitent Olivia shook her head enthusiastically.

Fire sparked from Ammon's eyes, "If your duties are not done by the end of the day Olivia, you will surely pay a penance." Ammon marched off towards home, Layton followed in his wake.

"Please Olivia, make sure you are home at a good time. You have tried your fathers patience a little too much recently," Sariah begged her daughter.

Olivia gave her mother a hug, told her not to worry, and skipped happily towards the town centre, her father's threat diminished in resonance with each step she took away from him and their church.

As she neared the town centre Olivia's nerves started to jangle. Her paranoia blooming she looked around at prying eyes attached to people who would be only too glad to report back to her parents with their judgements about her movements. In this town everyone knew everyone, and most folks enjoyed the schadenfreude of another's moral turpitude and the subsequent impact on devout family members.

Olivia passed Johnny's garage without going in. Rock and roll music seeped noticeably through the closed garage door. He was in. A ripple of pleasure ran up and down her spine. Olivia rounded the corner and ran round the block. She waited until the coast was completely clear then scurried up to the garage door and stepped quietly in.

Standing with her back to the door, her breath shooting rapidly from her nose, her eyesight adjusted from the bright sunlight outside to the gloomy garage inside. Johnny's denim clad legs poked out from under a rusty red Mustang.

Johnny's radio sang out rock and roll as Olivia, her white dress sashaying around her ankles, crept over, and kicked out at Johnny's feet.

BANG. Johnny's fright caused him to rattle his head hard against the underside of the Mustang. "FUCK," Johnny shouted as he scrambled to get out from under the car.

"Mind your language Mr Mann. There's a poor lil' Mormon gal present." Olivia smiled as Johnny's oil smeared face appeared.

The dimples denting Olivia's cheeks melted Johnny's irritation, though it would take more than dimples to sooth the big, angry, red welt that was now appearing on the side of his head.

"Livvy, you've managed to escape from the iron grip of your Overlord?" Johnny said as he stood up, wiping his hands on an already oily rag pulled from his back pocket.

"I have indeed, but you know there is no escaping ever from the all-seeing eye of God," Olivia feigned fear, looking all around her for the hand of God that was surely going to smite down this poor sinner. Olivia laughed and danced a little jig to the music coming from the radio.

Johnny made to grab Olivia to dance with her, "Woah there dirty boy. You can't come near this pure white dress with those dirty overalls on. My father is not stupid. One speck of oil on this dress and I am done for." Olivia danced away from Johnny twirling her dress around.

Johnny laughed, and a glint shone in his eye, "I'm going to have to take these dirty old things off then." Johnny matched his proclamation by grappling with the clasps of his dungarees.

Olivia shrieked, "Oh no you don't Mr Mann. I wouldn't know where to look." Ever so carefully Olivia, with her hands holding back the front of her dress, leaned forward, and closing her eyes she planted a long kiss on Johnny's oily lips.

"Mmmmm, careful you, you'll only leave me wanting more," Johnny said as she withdrew.

Olivia licked her lips clean and dried them on the back of her hand. "And one day you shall have more sir. But not today." Olivia whirled around and danced away from Johnny.

Johnny walked over to the dirty sink in his garage and carefully washed his hands and face.

Smiling and displaying his clean hands and face Johnny approached Olivia as she danced. "I'm as clean as a new whistle now my love. I can surely have at least a little more today eh?"

Olivia felt her body melting, "I reckon we can see our way to providing a little more joy today. As long as we are careful."

Keeping her hands on Johnny's chest Olivia allowed their lips to meet in a long passionate kiss. Johnny's hands wandered over her body leaving tingles behind wherever they went.

Oliva broke away, her breathing was short, and her head was spinning.

"So, you've been to your mad church again today?"

Olivia controlled her breathing, "Of course. It's what a good Mormon girl does. Is that not right?"

Johnny strolled over to stroke the Mustang. "Were they going on about Bring-em Young again? The Mormon Moses?"

"How dare you slight the good father of us all, you heathen." Olivia smiled.

"He's not my pa," Johnny blew his nose in his oily rag.

"Disgusting man," Olivia said wrinkling her nose.

"Yeah, but you still love me Livvy. Don't you?" Johnny smiled, full of confidence.

Olivia looked at the garage clock, "Well, all the love in the world won't be enough to save me if I don't make it home on time. I gotta go Johnny sweetheart." Olivia kissed Johnny one last time before she left.

Johnny couldn't resist patting her bottom as she skipped towards the door, "Come back tomorrow Livvy eh?"

Olivia checked there was no one around before she left the garage, she turned to Johnny as she trotted down the driveway, "Wouldn't miss it for the world Johnny. I'll come see you as soon as I get the chance to escape." Olivia blew Johnny a kiss before getting as far away from the garage as quickly as she could.

Olivia stopped when she was halfway home to check her dress was as clean as when she had left her father. With a mix of pleasure and fear she remembered Johnny patting her bottom as she left him, she checked and was satisfied all was clean. Olivia was unable to see the clear, oily, handprint that Johnny had inadvertently left on her back as they were kissing.

Every footstep she took brought her closer to home and it dragged Olivia inexorably deeper into darkness, even though the sun shone bright. Turning into the path that led to her homestead caused a writhing serpent of anxiety to flay around in the pit of her stomach. Bess, the horse Olivia considered her own, was in her usual field nibbling on a bale of hay tied to the fence, she stopped to stroke her neck and say hello. Olivia could see smoke rising from the farmhouse chimney, her mother would be cooking.

Olivia saw some dark welts on Bess's flanks, "Has that horrible man been beating you again Bess?" Olivia kissed her horse on the nose. "I always thought God was supposed to mean love Bess. If my father is so full of God, why does he behave like he is so full of hate?"

Knowing that time was ticking, Olivia turned from Bess and ran the rest of the way home. Running helped change the way she felt, it helped to keep her crawling fear suppressed.

Out of breath and panting, Olivia burst into the kitchen, "Hello mother dear," Sariah was, as Olivia knew she would be, cooking.

"Hi Livvy, did you get done what you needed to in town?", Sariah fished fruitlessly for information.

"Sure did mom. I just needed to see Ashtyn about a project we're doing at school." Lying had become second nature to Olivia, though being dishonest to her mother still caused her great discomfort. Her mother's question caused Olivia to contemplate exactly what it was she truly did need. Olivia was grappling internally with big questions about the rest of her life and about who exactly she was. She wasn't sure about a lot of things, but her every instinct told her the one thing she needed more than anything else was to escape from this house, her family, and her town.

"Where's dad?" Olivia sought a distraction from her thoughts, and information about the location of her father had a massive impact on her ability to relax.

"He's just out feeding the chickens Liv; he'll be back soon." Sariah continued cooking.

This information only caused tension to acquire a greater grip on Olivia's nerves. She grabbed a glass which she filled with fresh milk from the fridge, she settled at the kitchen table to drink. The back door creaked, opened, and in strode her father.

"How are the chickens Ammon?" Sariah asked as she carried on chopping carrots.
"Chickens are fine, and they are now well fed," Ammon stared at Olivia sitting drinking milk. "Why are you not helping your mother?"

"She's fine Ammon," Sariah replied for her daughter, "She's just got back. She'll help out once she has had her milk. Won't you Livvy?" Sariah asked with eyebrows arched in entreaty.

"Of course I will mother," Olivia smiled a most willing smile and continued to sip her milk.

Ammon busied himself hanging up his jacket and washing his hands. Pouring himself a glass of water he sat beside his daughter at the kitchen table. Olivia finished her milk in two gulps and jumped to join her mother chopping carrots by the sink.

"What's that on your back?" Ammon rose, the chair he was sitting on crashed to the ground. Olivia froze. Sariah bent back to see what Ammon was talking about. Faint but distinctly visible on the back of Olivia's dress was the oily outline of a man's hand.

His boiling blood fried Ammon's self-control, "You've been with him. I knew you would, you just can't help yourself, can you, you Sinner."

Still facing the sink Olivia felt her stomach churn, fear coursed through her system and frazzled her brain. She felt Ammon's presence looming directly behind her. He sniffed at the patch on her back.

"Oil." Ammon grabbed his daughter by the shoulders and spun her round, his pent-up anger that had been building for weeks boiled over. "YOU...... HAVE...... BROUGHT..... SHAME....... ON...... OUR...... FAMILY...... NAME....... FOR........ THE......... LAST.......... TIME." Every word Ammon shouted was rammed home with a vicious slap to Olivia's face.

Holding her by the throat with his eyes firing righteous anger at her; Ammon forced her to look him in the eye. "You are forbidden from leaving this house unaccompanied until you have renounced your wicked, wanton, ways and proven finally that you have accepted the word of God once and for all. You need to prove you have fully repented your sins."

Shocked Sariah stood back her eyes bulging wide, she knew not what to do. Her heart wanted to rescue her daughter; her mind was terrified to demonstrate blatant disloyalty to Ammon.

Ammon let Olivia go and his anger instantly abated. Shock took hold, he sank to his knees, he sobbed, he broke down. "Look what you've made me do," he rasped kneeling on the floor. His head sank into his red, throbbing, hands.

Crying hard Olivia fled from the house and sprinted up the hill beside the chicken shed. On top of the hill there was an old willow tree that she and Layton used to go to play around when they were children.

Olivia slumped down with her back against the old Willow tree, something vital inside of her mind had snapped. Tears rolled down her slapped red cheeks, she stared vacantly at a world she was no longer able recognise. In a trembling voice she began to sing, "*I had learned to call thee Father, through thy spirit from on high, but until the key of knowledge was restored, I knew not why.......................*"

Story 5 - Imprudence

Big Pauli finished off his can of Special Brew, he crushed it and flung it into the creeping corner to join all other empty alcohol receptacles there. He stared out of the grubby window of his home which was, at that moment, a tatty squat cited halfway up Princess Road in the very trendy Camden Town. The radio was on, John Peel was halfway through his nightly Fall half hour. Pauli voiced what was niggling at his peace of mind, "Anyone got any idea where them two numb necks are? I worry when they're out and about."

Pauli turned round to see if anyone in the room was listening to him. Barney was absorbed with his work of turning plain leather strips into sellable plaited bracelets. Matt was sitting on the floor ferociously scrubbing a pair of muddy white Nike trainers, in a futile attempt to restore them to their formerly pristine condition. Matt looked like he had recently consumed amphetamines. Kev was sitting on the floor in a corner of the room glowering at his reflection in a broken mirror. "Fucking wasting my breath talking to youse lot," was Pauli's summation of his communication endeavours.

"You know them pair, they'll be out saving minds and bodies again," Barney broke from his work to respond to Pauli. "And don't forget Pauli," here Barney switched from his black country accent to feign poshness, "Edgar darling is Oxbridge educated," before he dropped back into his native Wolverhampton, "As he likes to remind us often. I couldn't really give a fuck about Cambridge, but I do think that it probably disqualifies him from being a 'numb neck',"

"He fucking dropped out after a year," Pauli flopped onto their street liberated sofa, "And just cause he went to a posh school it disnae mean he's not a numb neck. Most of them posh pricks huv no common sense, you know that Barn."

Kev bared what blackened teeth he had left at his reflection in the mirror and emitted a low growl.

Pauli scratched one of the shaved sides of his head, "What does *he* think he is now then?"

"I reckon he thinks he's a lion or summat, he was prowling about the place roaring earlier," Barney filled Pauli in on the recent developments regarding the current symptoms of Kevins mental health disorder.

"If he brings another one of them mad cunts back here I'm fucking out of here," Matt grimaced to emphasise his disgust at the temerity of someone having mental health issues.

"And go fucking where?" Pauli laughed.

"There's loads of places I can go, and all of them are better than this dump. Them in that squat in K+C have got plenty room. I'll go there," Matt went back to scrubbing his shoes.

"They're all grafters Matty son. You're too much of a lazy cunt. They'd turf you out in a minute," Barney looked with pity at Kev who was licking his hand and rubbing it over his ears. "He's probably not the only yampy bastard in here either poor cunt," Barney sighed and went back to his leather work.

"Kin you no speak English Barn," Pauli struggled with Barney's colloquial description of madness.

"Bit rich coming from a sweaty," Matt gave up on his trainers and stomped out the area that was used as a living room.

"Cockney wanker," Pauli muttered not so under his breath as Matt left the room.

Matt's feet could be heard thumping their way up the un-carpeted stairs to his room on the top floor.

"Matt's a prick, but he's also right Pauli. We can't have another Kev here. The place would literally turn into a zoo." Barney looked to Pauli, "You opened this place, can you not have a word with Ed and Chris? Tell them to limit their mission to the streets only and keep the streets out of here?"

"Don't you think I've tried that already?" Pauli pulled a tatty paperback out of the pocket of his bikers jacket and started to read.

Kev started to purr.

Frowning, Pauli looked over at him, "Do lions even purr?"

"I dunno, he's probably just letting us know he's glad Matt's left the room," Barney guess translated.

"Him and me both," Pauli returned to his Knut Hamsun book, Barney returned to his bracelets, and Kev closed his eyes and curled up contentedly on the floor.

John Peel had finished bombarding the airwaves with wall to wall Fall and was now foisting Napalm Death on the ears of his listeners. Saturday night in the Camden squat ticked gently away.

Ed and Chris were out patrolling The Strand. Chris was dressed in his now bruised orange Hare Krishna smock. Ed was dressed in jeans, T-shirt, and a green cardigan.

Being a Saturday night, in mid-summer, central London was busy, lively. Various scraggy looking people were begging on The Strand, a few were ostensibly sleeping, covered by raggedy blankets, or grubby looking sleeping bags. Expectant eyes and warm welcomes from the homeless and begging community followed Ed and Chris as they headed towards Trafalgar Square. They were a well-known pair. There were a lot of very drunk people milling about, which, along with the usual throng of traffic, created a thick, soupy, hubbub of noise.

With Chris trotting behind him like a hang-dog puppy, Ed led the way to an empty doorway where he could study the presenting mass of inebriated humanity. "Let us rest here a while Christopher my good man. We shall see what gifts the Gods provide us with tonight."

"And you are sure this behaviour is not going to damage my spirit? My Karma?" Chris's frown spoke of the conflict he battled with on a daily basis.

"We have been over this too many times to count my poor unenlightened one. Wealth distribution is divine in almost all religions. Remember, I studied Theology at Cambridge."

Silently and gracefully Chris sunk to the ground, crossed his legs and eyes, and started to chant, "Ommmmmmmmmmm,".

"Scuze me mate, spare us a cigarette eh?" Ed found begging to be more successful if he altered his accent. The Essex drunkard duly obliged in supporting a fellow human being maintain his nicotine addiction. "Cheers mate," Ed smiled a smile only a very drunk person could have been fooled into believing was genuine, it positively radiated insincerity. Smiling a drunkards grin the Essex gentleman drifted off into the night.

Ed's smile slid swiftly into a sneer which was accompanied by rolling eyes as he watched Chris attempt to meditate his mind into serenity.

"*Gary's getting married in the morning. Ding dong the bells is gonna chime,*" a stag party weaved its way down Adelaide Street and round the corner onto The Strand.

"Bingo," Ed muttered as he flicked away his half-smoked cigarette. "Chris my faithful stooge, I think Thunderbirds are go."

Chris sighed as he rose from lotus to standing as if levitating. The stag party weaved closer. At a nod from Ed Chris started dancing joyously, he broke loudly into song, "*Hare. Hare rama. Krishna, Krishna. Hare rama.*"

"Wey, hey," the shout went up from the stag party, "It's a fucking Hari. Told you they were always here," Much jollity was loudly expressed, "Where's yer fucking mates ya twat. Hari's are supposed to come mob handed, innit?"

Chris danced around the stag party smiling, clapping, and generally encouraging them to join in.

Ed's eyes were scoping out back pockets for bulges, he spotted his 'mark' and manoeuvred his way towards him. Ed's target apologised profusely for bumping into him saying, "Sorry mate, it's this fucking loony," pointing to Chris. Pocketing his newly liberated wallet Ed assured the gentleman that there was indeed, "No harm done". Ed strolled nonchalantly back the way the stag party had come from. Chris danced and sang his way away from the stag, bowing to them as he left. The stag soon forgot about the mad Hari as the quest to find the next drink took priority.

Chris carried on dancing and singing his way down The Strand, once he turned the corner heading towards Adelaide Street Chris ran and quickly caught up with Ed. "I reckon we should make ourselves scarce from the West End now," Ed said as he hurried towards Cambridge Circus. "Let us go spread some cheer among the needy in Camden, Christopher my good monk. That should help restore your damaged spirit." Ed smiled a broad smile as the thrill of a successful lift pumped round his bloodstream.

Cash was still king in Ed's world, after emptying the wallet of its substantial cash supplies Ed discarded the wallet, and the rest of its contents, in the nearest dustbin. The wad of cash was quickly appraised, folded, and stuffed in Ed's pocket.

Taking the back roads, Ed and Chris marched with speed to Camden Town. They headed to their regular supermarket on Inverness Street. Ed grabbed two baskets, giving one to Chris to carry, he then set about filling them with rolls, cheeses, cold meats, and crisps. Once he had enough food, he took the baskets to the counter and bought a crate of Carlsberg Special Brew. "Could you give me a handful of plastic bags please my good man," Ed asked at the counter. Ed was a good customer, and he was pretty much given whatever he asked for, no questions asked.

Crouching down in a doorway on Inverness Street Ed and Chris set about making packages to dispense to their people. Ed had made sure he still had some cash on him, as this was the commodity most requested by his people.

"Now, remember what Big Pauli said Ed. We're not allowed to bring anybody else back. Kev is," Chris paused to try to work out the best way of diplomatically phrasing what was a touchy subject, "Challenging for the rest of the house," was the best he could come up with.

"Aww Kev is just a big pet really; the others are just too dumb to see his inner beauty." Ed waved a bag at Chris, "Besides, we will sweeten up Mr McLeod with a couple of tins of his favourite tipple."

Saturday night in Camden was just as busy if not busier than the West End, though with a different, more 'hip' crowd, but they were just as drunk, and their behaviour was in reality not so different. The first beggar they came across was one they knew well, "Spider," Ed welcomed him with a wide smile. His facial tattooing made Spider's nickname obvious.

"Ed. What you got for me tonight?" Spider had spotted the bags Ed and Chris were carrying and saw no point in exchanging pleasantries.

"Some victuals to make your evening more bearable Spider my good man," Ed handed Spider a bag. Spider grabbed a can, cracked it open, and took a long drink.

"Got any money Ed? I'm really hanging out for a hit, and I just got stung for a bag from Titch." Spider pulled the most pleading expression his face would allow.

Ed reached into his pocket and produced a crisp ten-pound note, "Will this help?"

"Aww, cheers Ed, thank you mate, thank you." Spider felt he had grovelled just enough so he grabbed the ten-pound note and shuffled quickly off in the direction of the nearest phone box.

News about the free booze and money was soon spread, and the bags and money quickly disappeared. Unfortunately demand outstripped supply, and there was an argument about the last remaining bag, but Ed knew the cans of Carlsberg would be required to prevent Pauli from harassing him. Ed kept a tenner for himself in case of emergencies.

"Shall we partake in a cheese roll before we return to our lodgings Mr Green?" Ed motioned to the wall that ran along the banks of Regents Canal where they could eat their food and watch the world go by.

Back in the squat Pauli heard a familiar voice approaching the door, with his usual gaggle of hangers on. Pauli shot up and opened the window, "Taff, here's the keys." Pauli flung his keys out the window, Taff deftly caught them and let him and his 'friends' in.

Taff's 'friends' followed him around because Taff made incredibly good quality LSD. Taff had dropped out of Cardiff University shortly after he learned how to make incredibly good quality LSD.

As he was coming up the stairs Taff ran into Matt coming down. Matt had heard Taff arrive; Matt was aware what Taff's arrival signified and he wasn't about to miss out.

"Awright Taff," Matt's face pulled a most sycophantic smile, "You bringing us some of your magic tabs tonight?"

"How do Boyo? I might very well have some freshly cooked produce which I could make available for you at a very reasonable price." Taff was smashed with drugs, but he was still a businessman, and he didn't care if people were ingratiating or not, as long as they had cash.

None of Taff's friends acknowledged Matt, and the snub was returned.

Taff slouched into the communal room, "Pauli my Celtic brother. How's life in sunny Camden? You still working at that tattoo place? What's it called?"

"Aye, Tats 'N That. I am indeed still garnering a measly wage from them Taff. How's things with you?"

"Productive Pauli. I would say things were being most productive," waggling his eyebrows, Taff tapped his pocket.

Pauli smiled and flung a tobacco tin to Barny, "Skin up then Barny, I think we have a party to start here."

Kev had roused himself from the floor; and was warily eyeing the new arrivals, grinding his jaws, and silently opening and closing his mouth.

Taff approached Kev somewhat cautiously, patted him on the head and said, "Evening old man, hope you're keeping well." It was part statement part wish that Kev wouldn't do anything too mad.

Kev responded by rubbing his head against Taff's leg and purring.

"So he's a cat today then?" Taff commented to the room.

"Nope, we think he's a lion. I've seen him roaring," Barny spoke while he was in the process of making a large joint.

"I didn't know lions purred," Taff said.

"That's what I said," Pauli concurred.

"I liked him when he was a monkey. Must have been costing you a fortune in bananas though," Taff broke away from Kev and sat beside Pauli who was still sitting on the sofa.

"Them two loons huv been told to feed him. He's their fault," Pauli said as he caught the tobacco tin that was lobbed back to him from Barny. Barny tossed the joint to Taff to light.

"Don't mind if I do gents," said Taff as he pulled a battered silver Zippo from his pocket. After a couple of puffs he passed the joint to Pauli, then did what he knew everyone in the room (except Kev) was waiting for, he produced his own tobacco tin, opened it, and let the room be tempted by the long strip of blotting paper acid resting innocently there.

"Much?" asked Pauli, his greedy eyes sparkling.

"Fiver a tab to you lot," Taff sat back and waited for the money to flow his way.

Sitting by the canal Ed and Chris finished their cheese rolls. They watched as a young goth girl ejected a recently eaten donner kebab, which floated from her stomach on a purple river of Pernod and blackcurrant. "What price dignity Chris. Someday human beings will surely wake up and realise the sheer pointlessness of alcohol," Ed said with condescending pity.

"Shall we go home?" Chris said mournfully.

"Do you really think there is going to be a greater show of dignity there Christopher?" asked Ed rhetorically.

Ed and Chris could hear waves of raucous laughter coming from the squat as soon as they turned the corner onto Princess Road. Ed just turned and raised his eyebrows at Chris who was plodding along behind him. As they neared the squat empty beer cans from the creeping corner started to fly out of the window, followed by howls of delight and gales of laughter.

"It appears they have plumbed new depth Chris," said Ed dodging a beer can as he stuck his key in the door. "I wonder which disreputable characters will be foisted upon us tonight," Ed pondered aloud as they trudged up the stairs.

Ed and Chris stood in the doorway to take in the scene that was presented to them. Pauli was trying to kick empty cans out the window and Taff was trying to rugby throw them backwards between his legs out the window. Every success was hailed by a manic cheer. Matt was lying backwards gawping at the flaky paint on the walls as if viewing a Picasso. Barney was waving a joint about making wowing noises as he viewed the trails being left from the embers.

Looking at Taff, Ed summed it up, "They're tripping". Ed smiled and turned to Chris, "Now there's a substance that's a whole world more worthwhile than alcohol. Shall we join them Chris? You could contemplate your attachments or something."

Ed waited until Taff had thrown a can unsuccessfully against the wall before he interrupted him. Ed didn't need to say a word, he just handed Taff his emergency tenner, Taff got the message. Ed passed a tab to Chris, then swallowed his. Taff returned to his mission and the revelries in the living room continued. Chris and Ed retired to the room they shared to enjoy a more peaceful experience.

Taff was normally not a bad businessman; his markup was phenomenal as he had a team that stole all his raw ingredients for him. Taff knew that students would steal anything for relatively little reward. But on nights like these when he indulged too much on his own produce his vigilance slipped slightly. Tonight it slipped badly, and he left a handful of acid blotters out on the wooden crate that served as a table.

No one noticed Kev spot the blotters. No one noticed Kev pick up a couple of the blotters to stare quizzically at them. No one noticed Kev swallow two fine quality LSD tabs. In around about an hour, everyone, regardless of how out of it they were, noticed that Kev had dropped acid.

Story 6 - Mania

Lightning strafed the skies, and thunder rocked the air, as a tropical storm battered the coast of a small oceanic island. Dr Oadwin, the islands only inhabitant, sat on a rock passively watching the wind-whipped waves pounding everything in their path. The driving rain and wild winds didn't qualify as even a mild irritant for Dr Oadwin. With his black clothes clinging to him like a wet suit he sat unblinking; staring out at the violence nature was wreaking on the place he currently called home.

Dying as dramatically as it was born the storm passed as the setting sun re-asserted its meteorological dominance and swiftly chased away the last of the clouds. Dr Oadwin's clothes steamed as he returned to the cave where he existed.

The sun never penetrated the darkness of the cave, this also didn't bother Dr Oadwin, he could see just as well in the dark as he could in the light. Content to let his steaming clothes dry on him Dr Oadwin lay down on the wooden construction that served him as a bed. Sometimes he slept, more often than not he just lay down with his eyes closed, recalling, in minute detail, his past ventures into the world of normality, of life, of humanity. He was acutely aware that the time for him to set forth into the wide world was due again, his roiling blood, his tormented mind, his intense desire, demanded it.

Dusting off the damp debris of the storm from his clothes Oadwin rose and sought out his bag, from which he produced a black leather box. Licking his lips hungrily, with a blazing fire burning behind his eyes, he produced a crystal globe the size of a large grapefruit from the box. This almost weightless globe, once activated by the warmth of Oadwins hand, displayed a map of Earth, every country pulsated a myriad of colours. A small, dense black dot signified the location of Oadwin, and his home, the rest of the countries of the world ebbed and flowed with all the colours and hues of the rainbow. The seas and the oceans retained their azure, blue, identity.

A yearning to destroy life and consume human souls permeated his every nerve end, his body tingled in anticipation. Scrutinising his globe Oadwin rolled it slowly from hand to hand studying the green, red, and grey/ black hotspots. The United States of America, one of his favourite playgrounds, was thick with every colour. Manipulating the globe with his fingers Oadwin magnified the U.S. He focused in on a sickly black/ green hotspot, floating on a sea of grey/ black, in the New York area. He magnified further and further until he could distinguish individual dots.

As Dr Oadwin rolled his globe from hand to hand another smaller globe had sprung to life, and was throbbing away in the pocket of Hannah Longbotham, a nurse, who was halfway through a night shift at Hammersmith Hospital in London. Discreetly Hannah took the globe out of her pocket. Her globe had only one colour, black, which was now swirling with a dense whirlpool at the centre, she knew for sure now that she was being summoned. Without delay Hannah reported to her head nurse that she was feeling unwell and would have to go home. Hannah grabbed her bag out of the locker room and made for the nearest toilet to lock herself in and change. Once she was changed she sat on the toilet, held her globe tight, and, feeling deeply nauseated, she sat and waited.

With his decision made, Oadwin pressed his finger on a dot of the most vibrant sickly blackish green. Oadwin closed his eyes as his body was wrapped in a rainbow-coloured translucent tube, his body rose and he rode in the rainbow flow traversing the cosmic plane through the physical world from his island to Manhattan, New York.

Oadwin could see the outside world through the thin rainbow gauze, but no one could see in. The citizens of Manhattan were largely unaware of his presence, though a few sensitive souls shivered when he flowed past, even though the night was middle of summer New York hot. Oadwin knew his nurse, aide, and co-conspirator, would be right behind him.

Oadwin flowed past a group of Wall Street traders who had just finished work, he spotted his target, Chet Adkins. He could tell it was his target by the intensity of his green aura. Flowing down an alley between two buildings Oadwin waited until the coast was clear before he removed his finger from the globe. Dr Oadwin materialised in the middle of a Manhattan side street; he was now physically present in America. Nonchalantly he strolled out into a busy, bustling Wall Street. Chet Adkins and his crew brushed past him; they didn't register the nondescript Dr Oadwin. A few seconds later nurse Hannah Longbotham, still looking sick and somewhat lost and bewildered, stepped out of the same alleyway.

"Nurse Longbotham, so nice to see you," Dr Oadwin smiled. "You look like you've seen a ghost, poor girl," Hannah shrank away from his sinister smile and focused on the ground at his feet. "I do hope I didn't whisk you away from anything important?" Dr Oadwin's attempt at sympathy lacked sincerity.

"It's fine Doctor, I was in the middle of a night shift at the hospital is all," Hannah kept her expression neutral and refused to make eye contact, she was too scared about the insanity she knew she would see there.

"Ahh the poor pitiful souls of Hammersmith. They will just need to cope for one night without your professional ministrations." Casually Oadwin followed after Chet Adkins and his colleagues as they strode down Wall Street. "The blond haired one in the pale blue suit is our…….," Oadwin searched for a suitable work, "……….. mission for tonight."

Hannah stared mournfully at Chet and sighed quietly; she braced herself for whatever the night would inevitably bring, she felt a vertiginous tingle traverse her spine.

Chet Adkins eye's tracked the passage of a deep red Bugatti Veyron as it purred slowly down Wall Street. "Swift one at the Bailey?" one of his colleagues suggested. The idea was met with the usual unanimous approval. Chet tore his eyes from the coveted car and sprayed his gaze around the women walking around Wall Street. He settled for gawping at a curvaceous blond in a short skirt and white blowse.

"Hey Chedy, put your eyes back in your head, you can't afford her," one of his colleagues shouted as he punched Chet on the shoulder.

"He's giving it a go at getting there though. If he sticks his head any further up the BSD's ass his ears will be full of shit I reckon," this comment, delivered by another colleague, was accompanied by an exaggerated licking motion.

"Fuck off dickbrain," Chet replied, "You'll be begging for favours after I go long, fucking asshole." Chet sped up, "I'm fucking thirsty, let's get a shift on, it's way past beer o'clock."

Walking into the Bailey Pub and Brasserie the traders nodded and smiled at those of consequence, and studiously ignored those of a lower standing. Those further down the greasy pole desperately tried to get a nod of recognition from the traders. With shoulders back and their heads held high they swaggered up to the bar and ordered a Coors Light and a Macallans each.

Oadwin and Hannah were assumed by all to be tourists, and therefore completely discounted and ignored. Oadwin ordered a beer for himself and an orange juice for Hannah. Hannah paid. Oadwin led Hannah from the bar to a stall where they could watch Chet and his friends as they quickly consumed round after round. Oadwin and Hannah nursed their drinks, for them their 'refreshment' would come later.

"Our friend is getting himself into the perfect state for a journey into the unknown," Oadwin smirked. Hannah dutifully smiled.

Chet and his crew were restless, they wanted different people, different places. They sought better opportunities to rub shoulders with bigger Wall Street fish, or perhaps even to chance upon an encounter with a perfectly formed lady. Decision made, they staggered towards the exit, Oadwin was right behind them, they were completely oblivious of his existence.

Two minutes and fifty yards after leaving the Bailey Chet felt an urgent need to obey the call of nature. "I badly need to piss," he slurred to his friends, "I'll catch you up". Chet loped off down an alleyway and relieved himself behind a large bin.

Chet shook himself as dry as was necessary and adjusted himself, ready to catch up with his friends. When he turned the figure of Dr Oadwin was but a few feet away from him, standing staring at him. Chet heard not Oadwin's approach, he was startled and angry, "What the fuck you doing, freak. Have you just been standing there watching me piss? Fucking pervert." Chet made to push past Dr Oadwin.

Oadwin sidled over to prevent him, "Awww Mr Adkins," Oadwin bowed, "No need to be so upset. I am not in the least bit interested in your urine."

"How do you know my name?" Chet was thrown mentally off balance, which matched the state of his motor skills. Squinting his eyes Chet tried to read Dr Oadwins facial expression, his eyes, his body language, anything that would provide him with some information about what was going on, and more importantly what was likely to happen next. This was New York, Chet knew danger was forever present.

Oadwin glanced behind him and was satisfied that there was no-one near enough to notice what was going to happen next. Hannah knew the signs, so she slipped her hand swiftly into her pocket and held her globe tight.

"I think we all might all go on a nice little journey together." Oadwin reached into his bag and grabbed his globe.

"What the fuck?" Chet stammered as simultaneously Oadwin grabbed him and held him, then pressed his finger to the globe. Chet and Oadwin were surrounded by a luminescent black tube. Chet screamed as he left the ground and flew up the black tube and onwards at great speed. Hannah was swept up behind them.

Travelling the cosmic corridor to Oadwin's island Chet was forced into face-to-face contact with his captor. Oadwin grinned as he tasted the stench of Chet's fear belching from his pores. Chet screamed. Oadwin laughed. Hannah rode silently behind.

Petrified and entranced in equal measure (he was aware that what he was experiencing was completely extraordinary) Chet watched through the thin black tube as Manhattan swiftly disappeared behind him. He watched the Atlantic Ocean toss and flop as they sped over it. Oadwins tropical island came into view, they were heading straight for it.

As they approached the island they slowed down, "Who are you?" Chet managed to blurt out.

Oadwin smiled, "I am probably your worst nightmare Chet my good man."

Even though he had recently evacuated his bladder Oadwins words, and the intensity of his gaze, caused Chet to let loose a jet of steaming hot urine, travelling just behind them Hannah got caught in the jet stream.

"Why me?" a terrified Chet managed to ask.

"I guess it's just the luck of the draw dear boy. Justification you have no doubt utilised yourself many times to excuse your selfish behaviour; as you shat all over your friends in order to propel yourself forever up the greedy, greasy, pole."

The trio flew right into Oadwins cave. Once they landed Oadwin shook his globe. It lit the sparse cave in a bright amber glow, "I want you to see how extremely nasty this is going to be for you."

"Who are you and how did you just do that," Chet waved at the outside in a vague attempt to signify the cosmic plane he had just travelled down.

"That's just one of my little tricks Chet. I have many more up my sleeve."

"What are you going to do to me?"

"I'm going to teach you a lesson. One that you will either never forget, or never survive; that will be up to Nurse Longbotham here to decide."

Due to the phenomenally dominant presence of Dr Oadwin, combined with Hannah's reticence to be involved, Chet had not until this point paid her much attention.

"What does he mean? Who are you both?" His fear fried brain was incapacitated. Chet made a futile attempt to stand up, running away was the only thing he could come up with, even though he strongly suspected there was nowhere to run to.

Hannah kept her eyes fixed on the floor, Oadwin strolled casually over and pushed Chet back onto the bamboo bed, "Just you shut up, sit back, and enjoy the ride." Oadwin started to march up and down the length of the cave, his hands clasped behind his back.

"Thing is Chet, you are obviously pretty much a complete shit." Chet just sat on the makeshift bed blinking as he watched Oadwin stroll and pontificate about his morally vacuous life.

"So when was it exactly that you were bitten by the green-eyed monster? Hmmm? Was it is when you were a senior? A junior? I would guess for you it was probably kindergarten and you just never grew out of it? Does that sound about right Chet?"

Chet was lost for words, he couldn't understand what Oadwin's angle was, he couldn't fathom what this most disturbing person wanted from him. Money? Sex? Contrition?

"And I guess jealousy just followed you wherever you went. Your best friend's girl at college? The star Quarterback? The singer in a rock band? Want, want, want. Does that sound about right Chet?"

Chet grasped at whatever straws he could think of, "You want me to change? I can change. Just get me out of here please. Let me go home," Chet pleaded, he was starting to cry, a bubble of snot blew out from one nostril.

"Yes Chet," Oadwin carried on ignoring Chet's plea. "You were bitten a long time ago by jealousy and envy, and now that particular chicken has well and truly come home to roost for you." Oadwin strolled past Hannah, "But, as I said earlier, your survival is not really up to me, my esteemed nurse and companion will have the final say on that." Oadwin stood in front of Hannah smiling demonically. Oadwin twirled and marched up to Chet on his bed, "But the time for change, I'm afraid, has long since passed. You should have thought about changing a long time ago. Perhaps the most obvious one would have been after you dipped your wick in your best friend's girlfriend."

"How do you know about that?"

Oadwin roared with laughter then switched to spitting with rage in a split second, "You fucking odious, snivelling, little cunt," Oadwins boiling red face was an inch away from Chet's pale white one, "You are all just so fucking predictable."

With Oadwin roaring in his face Chet lost control of his bowels. Oadwins nose wrinkled in pure disdain. "Pathetic," he spat as he marched away from the rank smell emanating from Chet's pants.

Chet turned desperately to Hannah, "He said you could get me out of this. He said it was up to you if I.........." Chet couldn't bring himself to say the word 'survived'.

Hannah looked at Oadwin, she knew what his response would be.

"Not yet I'm afraid Chet," Oadwin strolled back to the bed. Chet cowered back from him. "You need to know how this is all going to happen. You need to know exactly how you are going to die if, by chance, the cards don't fall fortuitously for you."

Slowly Oadwin approached the petrified Chet. Oadwins hand shot out and grabbed Chet by the neck. Chet felt a chilling cold flow spread through his body; he was completely immobilised. With his other hand Oadwin lifted Chet's limp arm and brought his fingers up to his mouth. Oadwin sucked one of Chet's fingers into his mouth, he rolled his tongue around Chet's finger flicking it onto his hard molars. Oadwin clamped his jaw swiftly shut. A howl burst from Chet's limp jaws. Blood spurted from his severed finger into Oadwins mouth, Oadwin drank the blood and ground down the bony, gristly, lump of Chet's finger. He swallowed. Oadwin smiled, blood streaked his teeth, "You get the picture Chet dear boy? I shall hand you over to my esteemed colleague now, pardon the pun by the way." Oadwin dropped Chet's arm and let go of his neck. Being able to move again Chet moaned, crumpled into a ball, and rolled about on the bed clutching his mutilated hand.

Hannah sat gently on the bed beside him and waited until his pumping endorphins calmed him down sufficiently for her to talk to him. Chet," Hannah pulled a pack of playing cards from her bag, "Listen to me carefully now."

Chet sobbed and held his bleeding hand, but he was aware that a critical point had been reached regarding his mortality, he knew his fate hung in the balance, he stared at Hannah his eyes pleading for mercy.

Hannah shuffled the cards and splayed them out, "You need to pick a card Chet. If it is red Dr Oadwin will set you free, I promise." Nurse Longbotham chose not to verbalise what would happen if he picked a black card, Chet was only too aware of what would happen if he chose the wrong colour.

Oadwin hovered hungrily over Hannah's shoulder. His appetite was inflamed as he watched Chet extend a blood-soaked hand out to pull a card. Chet looked at the card and howled. He dropped the King of spades on the bed as Oadwin, laughing victoriously, pounced on him. Hannah remained on the bed but turned her face away.

The bed bounced as Oadwin gorged on live flesh, Hannah closed her eyes and rolled with the motions of the bed as Chet's life ebbed away. The noises of Chet being eaten to death were grotesque and horrific, gradually the bed ceased to move, Chet's screams were silenced by death. A craving crept up from Hannah's solar plexus, her pay off time was close. She turned her head to look as Oadwin breathed Chet's departing soul into his lungs, as it escaped from his eyes. Oadwin closed his eyes in rapturous ecstasy as Chet's soul fed his immortality. Hannah's breath caught in her throat as Oadwin leant towards her. Oadwin held her by her jaw, and she opened her mouth to receive the dregs of Chet's soul when Oadwin breathed out. Their eyes locked in evil, eternal, collusion.

Story 7 - Vanity

Madam Adeline D'Espanet stepped back and carefully studied her reflection in the full-length Louis Phillipe mirror. Fluffing out her voluminous sunburst yellow skirt, she ensured it was dome shape flawless. Fingering her tight blond ringlets, and her mother of pearl double necklace, she made sure her bared collar bone was accentuated perfectly. Finally she made sure her matching bodice was sand smooth, and perfectly in place. Adeline practiced a bemused smile, satisfied with her appearance she breezed with confidence and grace out of her bedroom. Descending the stairs Adeline thought to check that the servants were preparing properly for her much-anticipated dinner party. There was a great deal of excitement and anticipation abound in Parisian society about tonight's dinner party, principally due to the expected presence of one Signor Gaetano Farussi.

Adeline swept into her drawing room and immediately rang for the butler. The wily butler had heard his Madam moving about, and had anticipated being summoned, "Is all as it should be in the kitchens Vautrin?" Adeline asked, deliberately not making eye contact with her butler, as she examined the drawing room for any imperfections.

"Yes my lady, all is progressing smoothly," Vautrin bowed his head in a demonstration of obsequious deference. "The cook has all in order as expected. Would madam care to inspect the preparations for herself?"

Madam Adeline had never trusted Vautrin and, though she was keen to make sure her party went well, having an excuse to dismiss the butler her husband had foisted on her would be most welcome, "No thank you Vautrin. I trust your oversight completely. Responsibility is completely yours."

"I shall retire then Madam and continue to ensure the culinary preparations are satisfactory. I shall also prepare to receive your guests," Vautrin smiled, and after Adeline had dismissed him with a nod, he bowed his way out the room.

Left alone Adeline ruminated about the various rumours concerning the main attraction of the evening, the aforementioned Gaetano Farussi. It was rumoured that he was related to King Charles Albert of Piedmont-Sardinia, though the precise nature of his connection was, like many other things where Gaetano was concerned, vague. His employment status was even more clouded in conjecture; and included nearly every possibility from the military to the church. More scurrilous gossip mongers posited theories suggesting that he was deeply involved in practicing the dark arts of the occult.

Adeline suffered a pang of anxiety and doubt regarding the possibility that Gaetano might turn out to be a somewhat unsavoury character. Then she caught a glimpse of the fluttering curtains of her Passy-Auteuil neighbours. Her dinner party was the talk of the town, and she positively revelled in this status. Whatever happened tonight there was one thing that was certain, she would now be considered of greater importance than her most bitter rival, Madam de Bargeton.

The doorbell rang, a grimace of distaste flickered in her face as she heard Vautrin welcoming General de Carnavant and his wife Nana to her house. Adeline vowed to confront her husband about dismissing this vile creature from their employ once he returned from his business trip.

"Charles, Nana. Welcome. How are you both?" Adeline smiled broadly at her guests as she offered her cheeks for kissing. "Vautrin, bring some refreshments for my guests," she added coldly as Vautrin relieved the General and his wife of their coats.

Charles cleared his throat, frowned, and blundered straight to the point, "So do we get to meet Italian royalty tonight then?" Charles had never gotten used to societal norms, and was not known for his subtlety; he was more comfortable when he was amongst fellow servicemen.

Nana came to his rescue, she patted her husband's arm, "Plenty time to talk about the guests later darling." Nana smiled at their host, "You look divine tonight Adeline my dear. Your pearls are to die for."

"Thank you darling," Adeline hooked the General's arm and led him into the centre of the room, she was keen to talk about Gaetano. "I have indeed managed to lure Don Farussi to my humble abode Charles. I am most excited to meet him. Aren't you?"

"Isn't he a Viscount or something? I heard he was related to the old King?" Charles looked about as animated as he could get, he was twirling his large, bushy, moustache.

"I heard exactly the same thing Charles. Though I have also heard many other stories besides," Adeline said, raising her eyebrows enigmatically.

Adeline heard more of her guests arrive as she chatted with the old General.

Newlyweds Francois and Martha Mouret were next to enter the drawing room; followed by the eminent journalist Emile Blondet. Emile was deep in conversation with Francois about the transformation of the boulevards of central Paris currently underway, "And I tell you Francois, the Emperor is leading the way in transforming Paris. We will soon be the envy of Europe if not the whole world."

"And no doubt you will be singing the praises of Napoleon III in your paper again Emile," Adeline interjected to remind him of her presence and his need to acknowledge her.

Emile laughed, "Unless of course there is something more important happens this evening Adeline," Emile bowed to her, "Which is of course not beyond the impossible. Madam de Bargeton will be positively green with envy."

Adeline smiled, satisfied with Emile's response, particularly at the thought of the anguish caused to her bitter rival. "Welcome to my humble abode," she said as she showered them with the transient butterflies of air kisses.

Next to arrive was the young journalist, Lucien Chardon. Lucien was astonished and overwhelmed that he had managed to wangle an invite to this most exclusive gathering. Lucien managed to achieve an unobtrusive entrance, he stood as close to Emile

Blondet as was respectfully possible in the vain hope of receiving some recognition as a fellow man of letters.

Close behind Lucien was Father Edouard LaFosse. Father LaFosse was generally invited to parties in order to provide moral legitimacy. Polite society were assured that any party with Father LaFosse present was completely above board and beyond reproach. Given the addition on the guest list of the unknown entity Gaetano Farussi, Father LaFosse's inclusion was considered all the more necessary by Adeline. Her previous anxieties were greatly assuaged by his presence.

Father LaFosse was a thin, bony man with an aquiline, hooked nose. His brown, almost black eyes perfectly conveyed the intensity of his opinions concerning the moral reprehensibility of the majority of Parisians. Father LaFosse was never more in his element than when he was standing in his pulpit in the Chapelle Expiatoire breathing the fire of brimstone judgement over his congregation.

"Looking forward to meeting Italian royalty tonight Father La Fosse?" General De Carnavant tried to engage the priest in polite conversation.

"Royal blood is no guarantee of a pure soul General," Father La Fosse was probably not the best person for the General to attempt polite conversation with.

"You're absolutely correct Father, pure souls indeed," the General blustered, then wandered off and stood beside his wife who was expounding on the virtues of treating your domestics well, to a plainly disinterested Adeline. Adeline was, at that moment, experiencing rising anxiety about the possibility that her star performer might just not turn up to her soiree. Being snubbed would ensure a slippery slope for her social standing.

The sound of the doorbell dissipated Adeline's anxiety in a burst of most welcome relief.

Vautrin announced the arrival of Gaetano Farussi. Emile Blondet, at that point, deigned to acknowledge the presence of Lucian, "So we do get to meet the Italian stallion after all, Adeline will be most pleased. Let us now see if he measures up to his reputation then, young man," Emile said as he playfully punched Lucians shoulders.

Lucian was lost for words; his mind was trying to process too many things at the same time. Lucian was dreaming of the credibility this night could bring him, never mind the column inches it would generate.

All the ladies in the room glided over to receive their kisses from Italian royalty, Adeline ensured she was first, "Welcome to Paris Signor Farussi. Or do you have a title you would prefer we use?" Adeline didn't waste any time before fishing for information.

Gaetano smiled, kissed both of his hostesses cheeks, "Signor is a good enough title to call me as any," with this he flourished a deep bow, "Any title sounds divine coming from your lips, of course, Madam."

The other ladies laughed politely and lined up for their kisses.

Emile noticed Francois Mouret's eye's narrow as his wife fluttered alongside the other ladies vying for Gaetano's attention.

"All women like a foreigner I'm afraid Francois, they just can't help themselves," Emile sniffed.

"Not my Martha, Emile, she's different," Francois stared hard at his wife, willing this statement to be true.

"Who are you trying to convince? Thee or me?" Emile smiled sardonically.

"He doesn't look much like royalty to me," General De Carnavant cast his judgement in an aside to Father La Fosse, who sneered and grunted in agreement.

Gaetano was dressed in the very latest fashion. His suit was, of course, Italian. It was tight in the arms and tapered to the waist. Taken separately his features would have been considered quite ugly, his eyes were too close together, his nose too short and squat, and his lips could have been thought to be too thin. However, when they were studied together, along with his cheeky looking dimpled chin, the effect was quite striking. His slim build finished off the picture perfectly, even Emile had to grudgingly admit that Gaetano did indeed cut a dashing figure. It was evident Gaetano also knew this quite well, and it was patently obvious he enjoyed the attention he was used to receiving from the ladies.

Vautrin had been standing for a while, observing the dynamics developing in the room. He lifted and banged a large gong, "Dinner is served Madam," he announced.

An amuse-bouche was waiting for the diners to commence their evenings indulgencies. Father LaFosse conveniently forgot about his habitually austere nature on these occasions.

Adeline sat at the head of the table and surveyed her small, but perfectly formed gathering, as they naturally arranged themselves around the table. Gaetano ensured he was seated next to Martha. Deciding how he would best enjoy his evening Emile ensured he was sitting next to Francois. "Our Italian friend seems to be getting on well with your Martha?" he said with a feigned air of innocence.

Francois ignored Emile, glowered over at Gaetano, and gulped at his amuse-bouche. Francois wanted nothing more than for this evening to be over as swiftly as possible.

Adeline directed the conversation, "So Signor Farussi…"

Looking Martha directly in the eye Gaetano interrupted Adeline, "Please do call me Gaetano, we are all friends here are we not?" Gaetano smiled, his strong white teeth almost flashing rays of light around the room. His smile set the pulses of the ladies fluttering and Francois's blood pressure soaring.

Fighting a rising flush Adeline continued, "So, Gaetano, please do tell us, what are your first impressions of Paris? Do we compare favourably with Rome?"

"Paris is of course the pearl of Europe Madame D'Espanet," Gaetano replied.

"Adeline please," Adeline lost the fight and a pink flush rose from her breasts, up her neck, and over her cheeks.

"Adeline," Gaetano carried on, "Rome is admittedly stunning and impressive. But Paris is positively heavenly, indisputably beautiful." Gaetano flashed his eyes at Martha as he said the word 'beautiful', a fact which was not lost on Francois, whose cheeks matched Adeline's for colour, but for a whole other reason.

"Have you been for a stroll on our new boulevards? I believe they might well be the widest in Europe," Emile pitched in with obvious pride.

Gaetano smiled at all the ladies, "I would need a guide I think. Are there any volunteers?"

Francois snapped, "It would NOT be seemly for any married ladies to be seen strolling the boulevards with you I'm afraid Signor Farussi."

Gaetano sighed theatrically, "I thought we had dispensed with formalities Monsieur, I'm sorry what was your name again?" Gaetano frowned.

"Francois Mouret, Signor. A name you would do well not to forget," Francois was grateful for the distraction of Vautrin who had just appeared to take away the empty plates. Francois was unable to think clearly. Vautrin sensed an interesting, developing atmosphere and he took his time collecting the dishes to see if he could detect, and exploit, the source of the unpleasantries. It didn't take long for him to discern precisely what was going on and Vautrin knew exactly what it was likely to lead to.

"I hear you have a new horse General," Adeline sought to direct the conversation away from potential confrontations, she tried desperately to reduce the tensions simmering away in her dining room.

"I have Adeline, an exceptionally fine Arab charger she is too." The General shrugged, "The only problem is, I'm afraid I am too old to take her out, but I have plenty strapping sons who will be only too glad to give her some exercising I'm sure."

Gaetano could not help himself, looking at Martha he commented, "So it's true? Paris is indeed full of fine filly's."

Francois exploded. Pushing his chair back he threw his napkin at Gaetano, "Enough, enough, enough," he shouted. "You have pushed me too far sir. You are a crude and rude individual, and you deserve to be punished." The diners were stunned into frozen silence. Francois continued to rant, "I demand immediate satisfaction. Dawn tomorrow. A duel. You sir, can choose the weapons." With this Francois marched over to his wife, and, rather roughly grabbing her by the arm, he led her away from Gaetano. Remembering his manners he sought to regain some dignity, he stopped at the doorway and turned to bow to Adeline. "My apologies Madam, but I just could not tolerate such outrageous and obnoxious behaviour anymore." With this he marched himself and his wife out the room.

Instead of immediately going to retrieve their coats, Vautrin went instead straight to Gaetano, "You will need a second sir. I humbly offer my services," he whispered to a shocked Gaetano. With this service offered Vautrin dashed off to provide the departing Mourets with their coats.

The stunned room returned to a noisy murmur, everyone studiously ignoring Gaetano. The pride, and possibly life, of a friend, and fellow Frenchman was at stake. Adeline's mind furiously attempted to process what impact all this would have on her reputation. Would society be excited and envious that such an event took place in her house? Or would she be judged as imprudent to invite such a scandalous character into her abode?

Two days later the following article appeared in L'Univers.

A Rather Tasteless Dinner – By Emile Blondet
I went expecting fine quality veal and some enervating company. Unfortunately, the only dish that was served at Madam D'Espanet's recent soiree, in her plush apparent at the Passy-Auteuil, was shame. Madam D'Espanet, a person I still consider a friend, was not the only innocent victim, French pride, and the dignity of our most precious French women were also gravely insulted. A man, I also considered a friend, stood up and was counted. Francois Mouret defended our honour magnificently, but he paid the ultimate price for it.

The cause of all this pain and indignity was a charlatan masquerading as Italian royalty. It was obvious from the moment I set eyes on him that no blue-blooded Italian could, or would, behave so coarsely in any company, never mind the company of fine upstanding French ladies and gentlemen (if I may be so bold as to include myself in that category), my experience of meeting this person has reinforced that old proverb that all that glitters is indeed not gold.

I blame not, (and would hope French society can be as equally forgiving), Madam D'Espanet for inviting this rogue to her dinner party. I was equally curious to meet such an intriguing person. Rather than holding anyone to account, instead I choose to celebrate the honour of the man who took it upon himself to fight for the dignity of our great nation. The name of Francois Mouret shall live long in our memories, a fact I sincerely hope provides at least some small succour to his poor, bereaved widow.

Another name I shall endeavour to forget at the earliest opportunity is Monsieur Vautrin. This man, I'm afraid, is nought but vermin. Though he was in the employ of the D'Espanet's as a butler, he took the extraordinary decision to offer himself as a second for the despicable Italian scoundrel (I refuse to use his name in print). I suspect that this poor excuse for a man robbed the Italian's pockets as he lay dying. One can only hope his ill-gotten gain curses his low life forever.

I ensured I attended the magnificent Bois De Boulogne on that tragic day. I

*unfortunately observed the fatal shots
being fired, and I can assure you all
that Francois Mouret died with dignity.
Paris is a poorer city for his passing,
but his example should inspire us all to
be prepared to defend our magnificent
city and our glorious nation against all
foes, at all times.*

*Vive la France and long live her
honour.*

The sun shone through the stained-glass windows
of the Chapelle Expiatoire that Sunday as Father
Edouard LaFosse came to the end of a long,
rambling, sermon, warning against succumbing to the
temptations of indulgence. Standing in his pulpit with
his blazing eyes spraying the congregation with
judgements, he took a deep breath and pronounced,
"Recent events in Paris have been a perfect example
of what I have been continually trying to impress on
you all." Father LaFosse looked into the eyes of his
parishioners, "I see through people, and I see the
mark of sin in every single one of you. I saw through
that Italian rogue Gaetano Farussi." Before
continuing Father LaFosse ripped off his dog collar
and tossed it behind him, "Farussi was punished, just
as you all will be, for consciously choosing the wrong
road. You must all now stop and re-evaluate your
pathetic lives." With his message conveyed as the
tocsin called, Father LaFosse turned, stomped down
from his pulpit, down the aisle, out of the door and
away from the chapel forever.

Story 8 - Control

This could be anywhere.

Jane E Drover stood staring blankly out of her office window. The city she considered her own lay brooding below. Jane's office was on the top floor of a multi-story block, so what little sounds the city generated never reached her office, at least not directly. One of the walls of her office was covered with an electronic map of the city. Flashing red lights lit up the map. The red lights were accompanied by recordings of conversations, this was all controlled by an algorithm programmed to react whenever a "key" word was repeated too often. The whole city was covered by a massive network of microphones.

The map was sparklingly active, snapshots of various conversations of concern fluttered through the air as Jane stared out of the window at searchlights probing the city. The searchlights served as a visual reminder to the citizens that there was nowhere to hide from the all-seeing eye, and the all-hearing ear. The real monitoring of the residents was, in actuality, achieved by more sophisticated and effective means. The searchlights shone down from massive watchtowers, that punctuated the wall surrounding the city, like monolithic exclamation marks. The wall kept people in and kept people out.

Drawing a deep breath Jane tore herself away from the window and strode over to her desk. As she sat down she pressed a button on the desk to bring up her slim LED computer screen, she flicked at the icons on the touch screen and the call went out to her five senior field agents. Each of the agents was head of security in their respective sectors of the city.

The agents promptly answered the call and sat respectfully silent, waiting until their boss addressed them, "Sit-reps now," Jane barked at the screen, "Central you first."

"All the central agents are armed and ready Ma'am. I've got undercover field agents conducting surveillance outside all target addresses. They report no unusual activity. There is currently no indication that the targets are aware of our plans Ma'am."

"North?" Jane barked.

"Ditto from North Ma'am. Agents armed and ready. Nothing irregular to report."

Jane sat back, expressionless, and listened as her other senior officers fed back similar situation reports. When they were done Jane let the silence hang in the air, she looked straight into her camera and spoke quietly, "We go at midnight tonight. All teams. We go in hard and apprehend everyone present in all target addresses. There are multiple confirmed breaches of The Rules connected to every single one of the premises we are raiding. The people connected to these places are all reading books, having sex for fun, spreading dissention, and discussing pointless things like philosophy and ethics," Jane's lips curled in revulsion. "They are teaching their children to think for themselves, and we cannot, CANNOT allow this kind of behaviour to continue. DO YOU UNDERSTAND?" Her voice had risen in volume as she spoke, and she finished her speech shouting at the screen. As one all her senior agents silently nodded.

As her passions became inflamed Jane felt extremely uncomfortable. She abruptly ended the video call with her agents. Turning off the flashing surveillance map she sat back in her chair in silence, and closed her eyes. Jane breathed deeply until her heart slowed and a steely calm once again regained control of her emotional state.

Composing herself, Jane re-opened her eyes and brought her computer screen back up again, she called her leader, who immediately appeared on her screen. Keeping her facial expression completely neutral she addressed her leader, "Roger. I hope all is well with you. I have just held a briefing with my agents, and I thought you would like to know that all is as it should be for tonight."

Roger smiled coldly, "Jane, I would expect nothing less from you. You're organisational skills and moral fibre are indeed beyond compare." Roger stared down his camera, "I wondered if you would be considering using the Übermensch in this operation Jane? It is an extremely large undertaking; raiding so many addresses in one night."

Jane blinked and paused, "I wasn't really planning to Roger. They've never been tested operationally. We don't really know how they will react."

"Might be the perfect time to find out Jane, and if they do turn out to be a little……..," Roger searched for an appropriate word, "…..overzealous, then what harm will really be done? It would send the deviants a clear message that we will not tolerate nonconformist behaviour in any way shape or form."

Jane knew an answer was not required; she nodded her head slowly "I shall see if the Übermensch are ready to participate now Roger."

"Yes. Do that please Jane. Thank you." Roger ended the call.

Jane was disturbed, she didn't like her plans being altered, especially at such short notice, but knew she had no option other than to do her leader's bidding. The Übermensch were a hybrid creation, half human/half machine. They were the pet project of the leader, and were designed to ensure his iron grip on the populace remained unbreakable. Jane had no issues about the aims of the Übermensch project, but the use of them in the field introduced a variable she couldn't predict the outcome of. Jane did not like unpredictability.

Once again Jane poked her finger at the icons on her computer, this time calling Dr Gleemen. It took longer to get through this time, but eventually Dr Gleemen's red face appeared on the screen. Jane took a more conciliatory tone with Dr Gleemen than with her agents. Dr Gleemen's connections to Roger required that she be treated with more diplomacy and tact than Jane would treat any other person, "Mary. How have you been? How's our Übermensch getting on?"

"Jane, I'm well. How are you?" Mary's desk was covered in papers and mathematical tools, Mary was rummaging for something.

"Just getting ready to round up a few hundred dissidents Mary, you know, the usual," disdain for Dr Gleemen's theoretical and intellectual occupation leaked from underneath Jane's words. "Roger would like the Übermensch to be used in the operation tonight Mary. Do you think they are ready?"

This statement, delivered so casually, got Mary's attention instantly, she stopped searching her desk and stared down the screen, "Jane. I *know* the Übermensch are ready for anything, I don't need to 'think' anything. But are your agents ready to manage them? Their training with the Übermensch has not been in the field, as it were, it's only been in simulations!"

Jane couldn't help herself, she bit, "My agents are experts in the field, they can, and do, manage every situation they come across. I know the Übermensch are untried, but as long as they have been programmed correctly then there shouldn't be any issues, should there Mary?"

Dr Gleemen smiled, and the computer screen nearly cracked from the ferocity of her expression, "There are no issues with programming Jane." Dr Gleemen returned to her rummaging, though she had clearly forgotten precisely what it was she was looking for. "Tonight it is then; excellent, it's about time my men got out to play. How many of them will you need?"

Jane did a quick calculation in her head, based on how many properties she knew they would be raiding, "I'd say five for each area should be sufficient. Shall I send someone round to pick them up? We will be commencing operations at midnight, so we have a couple of hours to mobilise your men." Jane watched Dr Gleemen nodding, "I shall inform my agents they will be having extra company for their raids. My men will know what to do."

"I shall get the Übermensch ready now," Mary looked slightly nervous now that reality was dawning on her. If the Übermensch failed, or malfunctioned, the consequences for her would be severe, "Send someone round Jane, they will be ready forthwith." Mary hung up.

Jane called her senior agents and informed them of the new situation. They accepted the changes with no questions asked, the Übermensch would be delivered directly to them.

Jack Jones sat in his nondescript office in the central region of the city. His computer screen slid down; he contemplated the news Jane had just delivered. Jack was tired, doubts about what he and his team had been doing with the dissidents had been building and had begun to plague him constantly, like a toothache. The people he had been arresting and interrogating had begun to seem to him not particularly dangerous. Unfortunately, there was no one he could trust to explore or examine his misgivings with. He had no option other than to lock his doubts away in a very secret part of his mind. Jack knew questioning the policy about how to deal with dissidents was nothing but a one-way ticket to The Factory. Jack was all too aware of exactly what happened in The Factory; and he knew no one ever left there in anything other than inside a very plain, anonymous, coffin.

Jack shook his head and sighed; he went to break the news to his team. He knew the team would not receive the news well.

For the field agents taking part in a raid was one of the few occasions in their monotonous lives that they did something they could get excited about.

Stakeouts only provided them with too much time to think; whereas a raid was an adrenaline fuelled blast. Raids were about disrupting parties and arresting people. Raids were physically active and involved intimate human contact, (albeit that the contact was normally of a violent nature). The atmosphere in the central HQ communal area was upbeat and jovial when Jack marched in.

"Listen up people," Jack hollered, which caused instant silence, every face turned to him. "We're going to have company tonight. Head Office are sending us Übermensch for the raid tonight. We're getting one for each premises we are breaching." Jack waited for the news to sink in. "We've all trained with them, so we know what they are like. So, just like in training, we let them go in first, and we neutralise anyone they miss." Jack detected the disappointment he expected from his agents. "We might also have to scrape up some mess if they get a little overexcited. Remember people, we don't really know how they are going to behave in a live job, so we need to keep our wits about us and focus on our primary objective. No one gets out of any building we go into unless they are subdued, arrested or dead."

Jack gazed round the room, "Are we all clear?" he demanded.

Muted murmurs of, "Yes boss," was the universal response. With his message delivered Jack left his field agents to come to terms with their reduced responsibilities.

Jack shivered slightly as he headed outside to await delivery of the Übermensch. The city was kept in darkness at night (apart from the searchlights) to discourage outside activities, the authorities didn't need illumination to keep watch on the citizens. There was little noise emanating from the city, as usual, so Jack could hear the approaching van containing the Übermensch coming from a distance.

The Übermensch were designed to be ruthless, violent, and efficient. They were supposed to be hybrid human and machine, but Jack's limited experience of them was enough to convince him that virtually all traces of their humanity had been effectively removed.

The van arrived, the handler jumped out and, sliding open the back door, he barked in at the cargo, "Right, we're here. Out now please."

One after another the Übermensch jumped athletically down from the confines of the van. Their physiognomy was recognisably human, but their arms and hands were modified with metal coverings, their fingers containing electrodes with the power to deliver debilitating electric shocks to whomever they came in contact with. The knuckles on their hands were reinforced with titanium should they need to beat people unconscious. Their heads and eyes were mixed human and machine, their eyes fitted with electronics deigned to detect heat and movement. The Übermensch were incredibly fit, tall, and muscular, they never tired. Their facial expressions were set, cold, and unreadable.

The handler pointed at Jack, "He's your boss now. You just do what he says. Ok?" Nodding at Jack he said, "They're all yours now. I'll pick them back up here after the op," and with that he hopped back into the van and left the way he came.

Jack was left with the cold eyes of five Übermensch staring blankly at him awaiting further instruction. Jack took a deep breath, "Follow me," he said then led them into HQ to wait for the operation to commence.

The now empty van that had carried the Übermensch to Central HQ drove past a furtive figure scampering in the shadows from door to door on his way to a friend's house. The few other people he came across on the street ignored him, as most people did in this city. Friendship was discouraged but tolerated, just.

Reaching his destination the furtive figure gave the front door a distinctive rap. A small, prematurely aged man with blue sparkling eyes answered the door, "Joe, did you bring the book?" he asked eagerly.

Checking carefully over his shoulder, Joe pushed past the elderly looking gentleman into the house closing the door behind him before he produced a tattered book from the back of his trousers. Holding the book up and beaming broadly, Joe proudly spoke, "Behold Bobby, the one and only Marriage of Heaven and Hell by William Blake."

Bobby led Joe into his sparsely furnished home, there were eight other people sitting around eagerly awaiting Joe's arrival, their animated chat ceased abruptly when they saw who it was. Joe scanned the room, "Are the kids not here Bobby?"

"They're in bed Joe," Bobby replied. "We didn't know what time you were coming. I'll go give them a shout now, 'cause they do really need to hear this,

this is going to be magic." Bobby scampered off up the stairs to the bedrooms.

Joe sat down in what was obviously the main seat in the house, just for tonight, Joe would absolutely be the centre of attention. All eyes in the room were on him, he held up the book like it was a precious trophy.

With three teenage children sleepily following him, Bobby silently crept back into the living room. Bobby sat cross legged on the floor, his children followed suit.

"Are we ready?" Joe asked as he flicked through the forbidden treasure. The answer to his largely rhetorical question was obvious, so he began to read aloud, "Rintrah roars and shakes his fires in the burden'd air,"[1] he began.

The flowing poetic words, and revolutionary imagery, held his audience spellbound and silent until he started to read The Proverbs of Hell. The power of the words was having an obvious effect, Joe's audience was rapt, their minds were spinning, thoughts firing. Bobby couldn't hold back any longer, he interrupted, "Read that last one again Joe," Bobby's sparkling eyes burnt with fierce intensity in his captivated face.

"He who desires but acts not, breeds pestilence,[2]" Joe ceded gladly to Bobby's bidding. Joe had of course read the book many times prior to this recital, and he wanted time to discuss and digest further

---

[1] From The Marriage of Heaven and Hell – William Blake.

these most magical words. Joe and the others were desperate to discuss concepts most foreign to them.

Breathlessly Joe repeated the proverb and turned to his children, "That's what's wrong with this world we live in children. We're forced into not desiring anything. We're punished relentlessly for doing nothing more illegal than just following our human instincts."

Further discussion was unfortunately stymied. There was no warning given, Bobby's front door just burst off its hinges. There was no shouting; the Übermensch just exploded in and leapt at the first person it saw. This was Joe. He was unceremoniously battered unconscious with a clenched titanium fist. The rest of the dissidents, including the children, were taken down either by electric shocks delivered from swift fingers, or battered prostrate by massive punches to the head. The rebels put up no fight, no resistance, in truth they were beaten from the first moment this monster stepped into their space, and they knew it. The whole operation took no longer than a minute. Jack Jones and his agents just stood blinking, shocked at the brutal, ruthless, efficiency of the Übermensch.

The field agents shook themselves from their stasis and started to handcuff the unconscious and the shocked supine. Once everyone was cuffed the agents started dragging or pushing the bodies out to the vehicle that was waiting to ferry them to The Factory.

Jack looked at the Übermensch, "Come. Your job here is done." The man-machine followed Jack and the last agent pushing his prisoner outside. Jack again addressed the human machine, "You go with the agents back to HQ, someone will come pick you up there." Without uttering a sound the Übermensch jumped back into the van that had transported him, and the team, to the property, somewhat reluctantly the field agents joined him.

Jack turned to the driver of the van that was ferrying the prisoners, "I reckon I'll walk to The Factory; I'll meet you all there." Nodding silently the driver jumped behind the wheel and took off towards The Factory where all the prisoners, including the children, would be meeting their inevitable fate.

Jack gazed at the vehicles as they sped off down the road. He turned up the collar of his coat, shoved his hands in his pockets, and walked off, slowly, into the night.

Story 9 - Denial

Acceptance is the price of freedom. [2]

Solans sat, depressed, in his rancid, tatty chair, distractedly picking at the frayed fabric around a hole, where decomposing stuffing was now poking through. Laughter, swearing, and tinny R+B music (played on a mobile phone), floated up to his top floor flat from the playground below. This would be the usual estate teenagers hanging around, killing time, the same ones that regularly made fun of him for being weird. They scared him.

Raising his hand slowly he gazed at the book he was trying to read; I, Claudius by Robert Graves. Breathing deeply he dropped his book on the floor and reclined his head until it lay on the back of the chair; Solans closed his eyes. *"Things are no better here. Maybe I should never have left Poland."* With his head being so close to the fabric of the chair the stale musty smell was strong. *"Why did I change my name? What was wrong with Belsiński anyway?"* Solans had changed his last name to Bell, as he thought it make him sound more English. The result was that the young kids on his estate called him ding-dong, while the older ones went for the more sophisticated Quasimodo. This disturbed him.

"I miss my mother. I miss Warsaw. But things really weren't much better there. It's obvious that the problem is me." Solans took ten deep breaths to empty his mind. Before he had reached ten his mind

---

[2] Narcotics Anonymous saying

had stilled. Solans directed his drifting consciousness, he visualised the Forum in ancient Rome, resplendent, shimmering in the baking Roman sunshine, most imperiously impressive. Solans, dressed in full Roman soldier uniform, was marching through the various cohorts of his legion, Solans was the Legatus Legionis.

Taking to the speaker's plinth, surrounded by his army, Solans mere presence caused the entire legion to swiftly lapse into silence. Solans raised his hand in salute, the soldiers saluted him as one. "Centurions, Decani, Milites," Solans spoke in a booming voice that rattled round the marbled columns and bounced off the walls of the Forum, "We return once again victorious from foreign shores. As a result of our superior force, and sacrifices, our magnificent empire has once again been enlarged." Solans extended both his arms to encompass his soldiers, "Thank you," he smiled magnanimously. His legion responded with wild cheers.

Solans wasn't finished, the legion attended again to his words, "Once again we have proven ourselves to be the most valuable, and feared legion in the entire Roman Army."

"And we've got the best Legatus," a legionnaire shouted out.

"The humblest Legatus," Solans ostentatiously bowed, the legionnaires roared with laughter. "For the time being, legionnaires, we relax, we enjoy ourselves, and we take some well-earned time for ourselves and our families. For when Rome calls again we will of course rally to the call, and we will fight for her honour once more. Legionnaires you are dismissed, go forth, indulge, and enjoy," Solans waved away his legion who cheerily dispersed.

Solans most trusted Centurion, Germanicus, waited at the foot of the plinth for him. Germanicus was extremely handsome, and he admired Solans immensely. Taking Solans by the arm, he whispered to him conspiratorially, "We need to go see the big boss sir."

"Claudius?" Solans replied, eyes wide with pride.

"The one and only," Germanicus could not contain his excitement.

Solans and Germanicus walked side by side, arm in arm, Solans could smell Germanicus's potent masculinity, and he could feel the urgent heat generated by their flesh-on-flesh contact.

Sitting in his armchair, in his flat, on the Pembury Estate, in Hackney, Solans breathing shortened and quickened.

"Perhaps we could have ourselves a little quiet one to one time before we go in and see our noble emperor, Germanicus? What do you say my trusted Centurion?" Solans said as he squeezed Germanicus's arm.

"Sir, we would be in such trouble if we are caught, inflagrante in the emperor's palace?" Germanicus let Solans know that the thrill of getting caught was incredibly arousing for him.

Claudius had a private palace in the Palatine where he received his most honoured guests. This was where Solans and Germanicus were to meet him. As they approached, a stony-faced guard was there to welcome them. He led them to an antechamber where they were to wait for their audience with Claudius. As soon as they were alone Germanicus grabbed Solans and pressed his hungry mouth to Solans impatient lips.

They were interrupted with a loud knock, and a ringing sound. Solans was thrown into confusion. The knocking continued and got louder, "Mr Bell? It's George. Your Tenancy Officer from Hackney Council. Are you in?" The door was rapped loudly once more, accompanied by another ring, ring, ring of the doorbell.

Solans groaned and stirred. Very reluctantly he rose slowly from his chair, "Coming," he shouted hoarsely. Sighing, he opened the door, "How can I help you, George?"

"Hi Mr Bell," George bounced into Solans flat and had a quick look around. "We're just doing tenancy checks Mr Bell." George craned his neck to see if he could see into any of the other rooms, "We need to check occupancy. There have been reports of sub-letting and of people allowing non-residents to live in their properties. Is it just you that lives here Mr Bell?" George smiled at Solans.

Pointedly Solans looked round at his empty flat, there was no TV, no sofa, only the battered seat, a small coffee table, and a shelf full of second-hand books, "Yes George it is only me who lives here."

"Would you mind if I checked the other rooms Mr Bell?"

Solans waved his hand in the direction of the door leading to the bedroom and bathroom, "Be my guest."

George smiled sadly as he checked the empty bedroom, "Fair enough Mr Bell. It's clear that it's only you here." George paused, thought and decided to broach a sensitive subject, "Do you want me to help you apply for a grant to buy yourself some furniture Mr Bell? A telly maybe?"

"I don't watch telly George. Thank you anyway." Solans stared blankly at George, "Is that all George?"

George nodded and moved towards the door, as he opened the door he turned back, "I'm always here for you Mr Bell if you change your mind. You do know that don't you?"

Nodding slowly Solans closed the door behind George as he left. Solans realised George had been the first person he had spoken to in over a week. The last person had been the DWP staff at the Job Centre. He looked round his empty flat. He never had any money, and he could never hold down a job long enough to get himself on his feet, which meant he could never get his flat to be how he wanted it to be. Solans didn't want to live how he was living but was resigned to his continued failure.

His poor mental health always impacted on his ability to function anywhere even close to normally. He wandered over to the filthy living room windows and stared down into the middle of the Pembury estate. He was correct, the teenagers hanging around were indeed the same ones that regularly taunted him. Solans stared with envy as they laughed, talked, and engaged with each other, he had never been confident enough to behave like that.

The sun was shining, and the day looked fine, the realisation that his isolation was becoming troublesome caused him to feel claustrophobic. Solans decided to go for a walk; if the estate kids abused him again, he would walk on by and ignore them. He knew they rarely left the estate, so the chances of them following him would be slim.

The lift was, of course, broken, so he trudged down the stairs and slunk along the wall managing to not be noticed by the teenagers, Solans was an expert at not being noticed.

Escaping from the estate un-abused Solans headed south, "*I don't know what to do. How am I to get out of this hole that I'm in. The same hole I've been in for my whole life. Pills don't work. Counsellors don't work. All they ever say is* 'Tell me about your childhood.' *My mother was useless, but loved me. My dad beat the crap out me. How does talking about that rubbish actually help me now?*"

London was a good place to live if you required, or sought, anonymity, and a bad place to live if you suffered from loneliness. No one looked even once at Solans as he made his way through Hackney and Tower Hamlets, he finally reached the Thames at the Tower of London.

Sliding down cross legged and gracefully onto a patch of grass outside the Tower, Solans adopted a meditative pose and gazed awhile at the HMS Belfast docked across the water at Southwark. Once he had calmed his mind somewhat he gently closed his eyes. Nearby a Mariachi band belted out La

Cucaracha with great enthusiasm, no doubt for the umpteenth time that day. Solans zoned the band out.

Breathing deeply Solans visualised a warship ploughing through the roiling waves of a dark and icy ocean, he allowed his mind to drift wherever it desired.

"Commodore, the sonar is picking up enemy activity approximately five hundred yards northwest. Radar is also picking up possible enemy aircraft approaching from the same direction. They are coming in fast Commodore."

"Thank you Lieutenant Orenda. Bring her down to four knots Sub-Lieutenant Lisotel. We won't be able to outrun them, so there's no point trying," Solans instructed his crew. "Captain Harrison, come with me on deck," Solans turned and strode off the bridge, and onto the deck which was slick with rain. Captain Harrison, with his hands clasped behind his back, solemnly followed.

The biting cold and howling winds didn't faze Solans, as he marched over to the prow of the ship. As he peered through a pair of night vision binoculars Solans addressed Captain Harrison, "I'm afraid we could be in very serious trouble tonight Captain."

Over the sound of the roaring ocean a distinct throbbing sound of fighter jets could be heard heading ominously directly towards the warship.

Solans turned to his Captain, "Whatever happens tonight Captain Harrison, we can still be damn proud of ourselves. We have destroyed our enemies' largest naval base and we will forever be remembered as national heroes." He turned to face the sound of the enemy planes, water sprayed his face, "Unfortunately though, we might now be just about to pay the ultimate price."

Captain Harrison stood steadfast, "We will go down fighting then Commodore Bell." There was an awkward pause, then Captain Harrison continued, "Might I take this opportunity to say sir, that it has been nothing but an honour to serve under you these past few weeks. You have been an inspiration to me, and I know I speak for the rest of the crew when I say they have valued your leadership also."

"We are not finished yet Captain Harrison. We will, as you say, go down fighting. Let's take as many of those bastards down as we can."

As the two leaders strode back to the bridge the enemy aircraft emerged from the black clouds. The bombs started to drop.

"Lieutenant Orenda, give the order to fire the anti-aircraft guns. Give the bastards all we've got." With the order given, the guns lit up the sky with rockets, one of the jets was hit. Cheers resounded through the ship. "Lisotel. Lock on to those pesky Sub's and blast them with our torpedoes," there was a glint in Solans eyes, he revelled in battle. Captain Harrison drew closer.

Sub-Lieutenant Lisotel fixed his eyes on the sonar reader, and set the target for the torpedo's, "Torpedoes away sir," shouted Lisotel as he followed their trajectory with the sonar reader. "Direct hit sir, but there are more coming behind that one sir. We are surely going to be overwhelmed."

"Fire at will," Solans shouted to his crew. Volley after volley of extremely advanced weaponry flew up at the aircraft and down to the submarines. Considering the odds Solans and his warship lasted much longer then they should have. The end, however, was inevitable. "INCOMING," Lisotel hollered just before the ship was rocked by a massive explosion as the rear of the vessel disappeared in a thick cloud of billowing black smoke.

"ABANDON SHIP," Solans hollered, "Man the lifeboats," Solans ushered his bridge officers towards the nearest lifeboats. Well drilled crew members were piling into the other lifeboats. The officers made it out. Captain Harrison and Solans were left alone with only one lifeboat remaining. "You go Harrison," Solans said, "I'm going down with my ship."

"With the greatest respect sir, that is one order I am not going to follow," Captain Harrison stood immovable in front of Solans. "The Navy needs you sir. We need you. I am not setting foot off this ship without you. I shall either live with you or die with you sir. Your choice."

Reluctantly Solans jumped into the last lifeboat, and they drifted off from the fast-sinking ship, Captain Harrison fired up the motor and they sped off to safety. From here on in they would only have each other for company and warmth as they sought to survive in a cold inhospitable sea.

"Mate!" Solans felt his shoulder shake, "Mate! You got any spare change?"

Floating in the lifeboat a confused Commodore Bell stared around for the source of this strange, disembodied voice.

"Oi mate," the roughness of the shake caused Solans to surrender the fantasy and open his eyes. He looked up into the beardy, toothless, face of an old, insane looking homeless man, "You got any spare change mate?" the man asked again. The stench of stale alcohol and cheap cigarettes wafting out of this persons mouth made Solans retch.

Pushing the homeless man away, Solans stumbled to his feet, "No. I don't." Solans was angry.

"Awright, alright. Keep your hair on mate," the homeless man bumbled away to seek his next opportunity/ victim.

"Fuck sake," Solans muttered under his breath as, resigned, he started to make his way off the grass, and away from the Tower. He glanced back longingly at the HMS Belfast as he turned the corner heading towards London Wall.

The day drew to a close as Solans wandered aimlessly through London. By accident he ended up in Soho.

Solans ignored the shout of, "Mr Bell," that he heard as he turned the corner from Moor Street onto Old Compton. The shout persisted, and got louder, "Mr Bell," Solans was confused, it couldn't be him, no one in London knew him, he strolled on and ignored the call.

A strong hand gently spun him around, "Mr Bell. It's me, George, your Housing Officer?"

Solans mumbled, shocked, he was not expecting to meet anyone here, least of all his Housing Officer.

"Come and join me and my friends for a coffee," George grabbed Solans by the arm, he was clearly not for taking 'No' for an answer.

Solans mumbled his dismay at this suggestion, but he could see that there was no way to avoid this most unwelcome social encounter.

Squeezing another chair round an already cramped table George introduced Solans to his friends, "Mr Bell, this is Simon, Russ, and Will." Solans noted that George's friends were very obviously gay. Up until that point Solans had only ever seen George in a rather cheap looking suit, shirt, and tie. Up until that point George had been just another faceless council employee, but now that he saw George when he was off duty, it was beginning to look to Solans as if George might be gay as well. "Gentlemen, this is Mr Bell, one of my most beloved tenants."

"I think we might leave you two love birds to it, "Simon said as he rose and motioned for Russ and Will to join him. Simon had read George's intentions. Solans face blazed red. George's face blazed red too, but he didn't try to persuade his friends to stay.

"So what are you doing in Soho Mr Bell? I've never seen you here before?" George sipped at his coffee.

Solans blinked, his brain was trying to process too many things, and his emotions had become like a tornado, he was confused, "You'd better call me

Solans I think George. This Mr Bell thing is just sounding too formal for here." Solans looked around him at the people laughing, dancing, and singing in the street.

George laughed, "Ok. But when we are back on the Pembury it's back to the Mr Bell and George the Housing Officer. But tonight we can let our hair down a bit I think? Let me get you a coffee." George bustled away into the coffee shop leaving Solans to regain some composure.

Returning with a coffee for Solans, George sat and smiled, "I hope you don't mind me asking Solans, but are you happy? It's just that, sometimes you look a bit depressed to me. And that is coming from one who knows, Mr Bell." George slipped back into the formal as he was aware he was asking Solans a very personal question.

Solans didn't know what to say, "I don't really know George. How do you define 'Happiness'?"

"I suppose it is just being comfortable in your own skin." George took a deep breath and ploughed on, "Which I myself wasn't, previously. I'm asking you about this because, partly it's my job to help you, but I'm also asking because I care Solans. And I think I have been where you are now." George looked Solans directly in the eye when he said this. Solans felt a tingle go up his spine and he wanted nothing more than for the earth to just open up and swallow him whole.

George carried on, "A few years ago I was in a very similar situation to what I find you in. I was alone, and I was very, very depressed, Solans. I literally couldn't get out of bed some days. I didn't wash, eat, or even dare to set foot outside my house."

Solans was drawn in by Georges confession. George didn't look like the kind of person who was depressed. Solans curiosity was piqued, "Do you mind if I ask how you got yourself out of it?"

George didn't miss a beat, "Self-acceptance Solans. I had to accept myself for who I was, a gay man."

The whirlwind of uncomfortable emotions returned with a vengeance to Solans body.

George carried on, "It wasn't easy, and even today I find the best way for me to live is to just take things one day at a time. I still have good days, and bad days. The answer for me was to not sweat the big things. Stop looking for the big answers, and to just focus on the simple things. I had to just start caring for myself, and I had to learn that I was worth caring for. It's a hard lesson to learn."

Tears started to well up in both Solan's and George's eyes. Solans pushed the feelings down. George let the tears flow.

Solans felt like he was breaking from within, his voice cracked, "I suppose I could maybe do with a bit of help."

George stood, "I'm here for you Mr Bell. I'll help get you through this and out of the hole you are in." George held out his hand, "I'll walk you home Solans."

Solans looked at Georges hand, his vision tunnelled, his guts churned, he felt things he had not felt in years, he felt scared, excited, ashamed, but ultimately he recognised that perhaps here at least lay some form hope. It felt like it might just be a risk worth taking, Solans slowly reached out his hand so George could help him stand up.

Story 10 - Pain

Fucking bitch.

What do I give a fuck for any of them pricks she's talking about? They're all her fucking mates, not mine. Not one fucking word about what she done. No apology, nothing. And just to make it a perfect clusterfuck of a morning, I get a parking ticket at the same time. Who the fuck even writes letters in this day and age? Fucking bitch.

This place is a mess. I can't be fucked eating anyways. Why is she not here? What did I do? What did I not do? I worked day in day out, and I never once held out on her. Gave her every penny I earned, near enough. And she goes and does that to me? I'm not going to fucking cry, not for that bitch.

Fuck it, I'm going to the bookies. God I stink. I can't be arsed showering. I'll just give myself a spray with this. Fuck, I've no clean socks. Sniffs. *They'll do. Right, have I got everything? Keys? Wallet? Fuck this shit hole, I'm out of here.*

If I bump into that prick Adam I'm gonnie fucking kill him. I'll be like, "Hello Adam. Long-time no see. Fucked anybody else's girlfriend lately?" *And he'll be like,* "Stu. Pal. I'm really fucking sorry mate. I really didnae mean to fuck you around." *Fucking poof. I'll no even respond to that I'll just fucking stick the heid on him. It'll feel so fucking brilliant to feel his nose mash up fae the pounding he'll get from my heid. I'll fucking deck the cunt and teach him a lesson he'll not forget. No one fucks with me. No-one!*

And if I see that cow, I'll no even speak to her. I'll just look down my nose at her like she's shite on my shoe, and not even worth bothering about. She'll be like shouting at my back as I stride down the street, "Stuart, Stuart, please, please forgive me. Let me come back to you." *I'll just fucking blank her and keep walking, my head held high. I won't let her see she's got to me. Hope that twat Adam has given her crabs, he looks like he's loupin'. Hope there's no cunt I know in the bookies, I really can't be arsed talking to anyone.*

"Two pound each way accumulator on them three nags then Jim."

"Done mate. How you doing Stu? How's life?"

"I'm awright Jim. Can't complain."

"And if you did we widnae care anyway."

"Aye, funny Jim."

Right. Ten minutes till the first race. Hope no cunt in here tries to talk to me. I can't be arsed with that lot today. C'mon Jokerman, give me a result, today of all days I could do with a bit of luck. Should be about £250 if all three win. Fuck, this place is miserable, full of smelly, grey, old men. Is that me now? Is that where I'm heading? Is that why she dumped me? Probably is. I'm just a big fucking nothing. Going nowhere fast. My dad was right, and all my teachers. It's no wonder she went with that Adam. His cock's probably bigger than mine n'all, and he's better looking. Cunt.

I don't fucking believe it, fell at the first fence. Fucking typical. I shouldn't have bothered getting out of bed this morning. Not really any point in going to bed either mind you, I've not slept right for days now. Don't want to be up. Don't want to be here. Don't want to be at home. Don't know where the fuck I'm supposed to be. I wish it was Monday and I could just go to work. Who the fuck ever wishes he could go to work? That's how fucked up all this is. I wish my heid would just shut the fuck up and stop tormenting me. I can't stop imagining her riding that fucking prick.

"You were right first time Jim. I have been done. Fucking donkey fell at the first. I'm off. See you later Jim."

"Laters Stu. Take it easy fella."

I suppose I better go get something to eat.

Maybes now she's gone I can get jiggy with someone else? Someone better than her. Wee Sarah at work is a bit of alright, I've always had a thing for her. I'd love to see the look on that bitch's face if she seen me striding out with wee Sarah. Sarah would never look twice at someone like me though. Pretty sure no one would have anything to do with me right now, I'm a mess.

"Slice, egg and tottie scone roll please love."

See? Even that old bag behind the counter didn't smile at me, and she's a pure boot. I always was an ugly cunt, even at school. Took me forever to pop my cherry. Wee Sarah would just laugh in my face if I tried it on with her. I'm not even sure how you're supposed to ask someone out these days. Do you just send them a text or what?

"Awright Stu?"

"How do Tam?"

"I'm awright. How you getting on?"

"Not bad Tam, you know, the usual, same shite different day."

"You still at Plaster, Optics and Electronics Stu?"

"Aye, for my sins. What about you? You working?"

"Naw. Still on the buroo. Do you know if there's anybody hiring? I'm fucking stony."

"Naw, Tam. Toon went to shite since the yards closed. Nothing happening anywhere that I've heard, been the same story for years now. And trust me Plasters is shite work."

"Well. If you hear of anything, give me a shout will you?"

"Aye, Will do Tam. See you around eh?"

Can't believe I've been at Plasters for three years now. I suppose it's better than nothing. But If I had a real man's job I bet she wouldnae have left me. How do they expect an experienced welder to get any job satisfaction soldering? Fucking soldering? No wonder I haven't been myself with her. Soldering crappy computer chips is not a real man's job, I used to build ocean going liners for fucks sake.

Fuck it, I'm going to the pub, see if there's any of the boys there. Cammy always gives me a laugh, and Shug is awright most of the time. Kenny's been bugging the shite out of me these days though. Always going on about all the burds he's had. If he starts any of that shite today, I'll just tell him straight to shut the fuck up. We can all pull any old burd if we want to. I just don't want to.

Who am I kidding? I'm fucked. I'm jealous, and I fucking hate him for it. I'll just blank him. Maybe's he'll not be there anyways.

I'm tired. Maybe a drink will help me sleep. Just to not be conscious for a few precious hours, to not have to listen to my fucking head going over and over the same shite, again, and again, and again, I'd give anything.

"Pint of heavy please Cathy."

"Be right with you pet."

Can't see any of the boys.

"Any of the boys been in today Cathy? Cammy? Shug?"

"There you go pet. There's been no sign of any of them yet. It's early doors though Stu. They might turn up yet."

Great. Now I've got to sit in a grotty pub, drinking, on my own.

Ten years. Can't believe she just flushed ten years down the lavvy. For him? It's just as well we've no kids. Maybe that was it? Was probably me that couldn't give her kids anyways. Couldn't even be bothered shagging her at the end. What kind of fucking pathetic excuse for a man am I. Fucking piece of shit, cunt, cunt, cunt.

"You awright pet? You don't seem to be your usual self?"

"Naw. I'm fine Cathy, my line went down in the bookies is all. Pissed me off no end."

"Want another?"

"Aye. I'll huv one more, see if any of the lads turn up. Give us a large Jamesons as well Cathy."

"Will do, party animal."

"Aye, that's me alright, living life in the fast lane."

So fucking tired, I'm going home. I'll get a couple of hours kip, hopefully. Surely with a wee drink in me my head will just shut the fuck up and let me sleep for a bit. Then I'll grab a shower and go back to the pub and meet the boys.

Everywhere I go in this town reminds me of her. The bus stop where we spilt our curried chips everywhere, drunk as fuck, and I nearly made her piss herself laughing cause I was pretending to eat them off the floor. The burd in the hairspray advert with the same smile as her. And of course our house where everything smells of her, was hers, and was bought by her. Fuck, no wonder I can't stop thinking about her. As soon as I'm in the front door all I can see is her.

Right. I just need to not think about her. Or about how she fucked me over...............

Just drift away, and get a couple of hours of blessed unconsciousness……………....

I need to not think about her……………………………………

Please? Just for a bit……………………………………………

Fuck……………………………………………………… …………..

I cannie fucking do it. My fucking head just will not stop. Where the fuck is this gonnie end up? I'm gonnie end up going mad, is where this is going to end up. People cannie survive without sleep! I cannie survive without sleep. How am I gonnie know if my mind just snaps? Will I know I've gone mad? Or will I just wake up in a loony bin and not know how I got there? Or what I did? What if I do something really stupid? What if I kill myself…………………..?

Maybe I should kill myself?

How?

Jump off a tower block? Fuck no. Far too messy.

Razor blades? Noooo, far too painful.

Pills? Too liable to go wrong.

Jump in front of a bus? Or a train? Probably be both messy and painful.

I've not even got the bottle to kill myself. I just must be the most useless prick I know.

Shit in a bucket, this is fucking relentless. So what am I supposed to do? Just sit here until I go mad..?

Fuck it. I'm going back down the pub.

I'm going to get fucking leathered tonight. I'm going to drink myself unconscious. With any luck I'll bump into that cuntface Adam when I've had a few bevvies in me. I'll make a fucking mess of that pretty boy face of his. His own mother won't want to kiss him after I'm finished with him.

"You back already pet? Pint of heavy?"

"Can't have too much of a good thing Cathy. Aye, pint of heavy please love."

"Stu, me old mucker. How you doing? Cathy said you were in earlier."

"Awright Cammy. I popped in earlier for a little snifter, yes. You want a pint?"

"Does a bear shit in the woods?"

"Pint of lager as well Cathy love."

"Better make that three Stu. Shug and Kenny have just bowled through the door. Looks like they've been oiling themselves at another fine hostelry afore joining us."

"Hey, it's the two old men. How long youse two been here?"

"I've just got back from earlier, and Cammy was here when I got here Kenny." *Bastard. I was hoping to get off without seeing him tonight. Ach what do I care, I'm getting fucked out of my head no matter what.* "Youse lot fancy a wee whisky?"

"Woah, slow down tiger. It's a bit early for shorts is it not?"

"Since when huv you been Mr Captain Sensible Cammy? I feel in the mood for a party, is all, I'm letting my hair down."

"Is that cause the missus hus left you Stu?"

Cunt. He just couldnae wait to get that one in. Next it'll be all about who he's shagging and who he wants to shag. "I'm relieved she's gone to be honest with you Kenny. She was a fucking pain in my neck. Cramping my style you know?"

"Aye. And you are indeed famed about town for your stylish ways my friend."

"Why thank you Shuggy. And one could also very much say the same about you." *You can just go fuck off with your mate Kenny if that's the fucking tone you're going to take with me ya wee cunt.*

"Joking apart though Stu, are you sure you're ok about her? Youse two were an item for ages mate?"

"Aye Cammy. I'm much better off without her. Your round then Kenny?" *Make mine a fucking double 'n all ya prick.* "Make them large whiskies this time eh Kenny?"

"Whatever you say batman. Three lagers. One heavy and 4 large Jamesons Cathy eh?"

"Coming up pet."

"C'mon outside for a fag Stu."

"Good thinking Cammy. I'm gasping for a smoke."

"You stay here with Kenny, Shug. When me and Stu get back you and Kenny can go. Someone needs to keep an eye on the bevvy eh?"

"Aye, Cammy. You're right. It's just as well one of us is thinking straight."

Nicely done Cammy my man. Keep them two out the way, they're bugging the fuck out of me.

"You had something to eat today Stu?"

"I had a slice roll earlier Cammy. That'll do me all right."

"Might want to take it easy with the bevvy tonight Stu. You don't want to end up doing something stupid you know."

Where's he going with this. "It's always either you or Shug that end up in the cells anyway Cammy my man. Old Stu is always careful. You know that."

"Aye. It's handy hanging out with Shug. He's too fucking stupid to know when to leg it. Gives the Polis an easy nab. I've been thinking a bit about changing my evil ways these days. I've been doing quite a lot of thinking to be honest with you. My trouble has always been I've never really took much care of myself, never have."

What the fuck is he talking about?

"And don't buy into all this macho Kenny crap. He's just as hard on himself as the rest of us. But we, I, cannie just sit around and wait for someone to pop up and care for me, I need to start doing it for myself. Same with you Stu."

I'm not liking this much. Where the fuck is he going with all this shite. I don't fucking need this right now?

"Stuart. You need to let it go pal. I mean with the tears Stu. Don't hold them in. Don't push it down. We all do that far too much. It's not right. It's not good for us. You need to start letting it out Stu."

I don't need this. Fuck. Maybes I do need this. Fuck. I don't know what I need. I don't know how to do it. How am I supposed to let go?

"Just stop holding on Stu. Trust me. Come here ya daft prick."

Cammy did something that doesn't usually happen in Scotland between men. Cammy gave Stuart a warm, sincere, hug. Stuart was powerless to prevent himself starting to let go. Tears welled up in Stuarts eyes and started to flow freely out. From that moment on the emotional release unlocked Stuart's ability to heal.

Hey ho.

There is a connection.

The End

Plus One - Dryad

Dryad

Let me relay a curious incident that has had quite the most profound effect on me.

I am a 42-year-old man, and prior to the day of the aforementioned incident, I would have said I had lived a fairly standard, humdrum life. I would only have ever described myself as "ordinary" if asked. In every way, I was by nature, sceptical. I don't believe in mystics, mediums, or fortune tellers.

I would never have discussed this, or admitted it in public, but I had also never been one hundred percent certain about the existence of God. Despite what the Church said, I had my doubts. I did care deeply about appearances though, so, I used to go to church, religiously, every Sunday, just in case. I practiced the art of what gamblers would have described as "hedging your bets".

By profession I was an accountant, I dealt in facts and figures, which naturally caused me to lean towards conservatism and prudence. I had an attitude to risk taking and security that I would have described as healthy. I live in comfortable, austere lodgings in Chepstow Villas, Notting Hill, London. I was, and still am, single, by choice, and look most likely to remain so.

As for the day in question. It happened as I was walking home one fine spring night. I was strolling down Pembridge Road from Notting Hill Gate underground station, minding my own business as usual. Flocks of birds accompanied me in my perambulations with the most pleasant warbling. Sprays of daffodils and crocuses decorated the tidy gardens of the ivy clad houses of my neighbourhood. Spring was most positively in the air, and I was feeling most jolly.

I remember I stopped to inspect an unusual looking plant, that had produced a profusion of the most wonderful blue flowers. The flowers were curiously shaped, they vaguely looked like small humans; they resembled an army of blue soldiers marching towards some strange horticultural war. Feeling so full of the joys of spring I stopped to sniff the flowers. They had no aroma whatsoever, I remember being rather disappointed, as I was expecting a rich heady smell from such a spectacularly beautiful flower. My momentary displeasure, however, did not puncture my good humour for long.

As I continued on my journey, turning into Chepstow Crescent I started to feel very peculiar indeed. My vision started to tunnel, and I completely lost all peripheral vision. Sounds seemed to fragment into their constituent parts, and I became conscious that everyday sounds had a structure to them that was ordinarily hidden from me (and, presumably, others). It sounds absurd to say so, but I could now taste sounds. Noises that had surrounded me all my life now had their own particular flavours.

This, of course, struck me as most disturbing, and not just a smidgen frightening. Little did I know then that things were going to get dramatically more bizarre before this day was out.

Somewhat hesitantly I continued on my journey home. Turning onto Chepstow Villas I noticed that there were no people around. Now, this was the middle of rush hour, in one of the most populous cities in the world. The streets of London are never empty at any hour. Having no-one around during rush hour is unheard of. I also became aware that there was an abundance of strange cats roaming around. Let me be clear, the cats themselves weren't particularly strange, they all looked like common or garden moggies to me. But I had lived for a number of years on Chepstow Villas, I knew, at least by sight, most of the neighbourhood pets and strays. These cats were all, unfamiliar.

I felt light, my mass seemed to drop away. As I continued to pound my way gingerly home I became conscious that the road underneath my feet felt, well, it simply felt like it was not there. I looked down, largely to check that the pavement did indeed still exist, which of course, It did. But my steps were not falling onto the pavement, instead they were floating just above the paving slabs. It appeared to be that I was levitating.

To this day, I still cannot explain what happened to me, but I can assure you that what I experienced that day was as real to me then as the seat I am sitting on now, writing this record, is.

I tried to convince myself that my mind was playing tricks with me. I was terribly dismayed that my mind would do this to me, but it was an infinitely more palatable explanation than the alternative. People cannot defy the laws of gravity. I remember thinking that if I lost my mind, at least there would be a small possibility that I could regain my sanity again, at some point. The laws of gravity, however, are immutable, they simply cannot be breached. It is law.

As I got nearer to home my predicament became harder and harder to ignore, I was rising with nearly every step. It was as if I were climbing an invisible stairway. I was now eternally grateful that there wasn't a soul around. My situation would have been excruciatingly embarrassing, and quite impossible to explain. The scavenging cats didn't seem to care.

I "stood" in mid-air and looked all around me. I started to become swept away by a feeling of deep euphoria. Perhaps I really was flying? Could I be like the birds and take flight at will? Could I soar with the clouds and see what they see? Could it be, that while the Americans experimented with their new-fangled machines in order to achieve flight, I had attained their goal with just my flabby middle-aged body? I tried to fly. All that happened was that I ended up flapping about in the mid-air in a most undignified manner. I achieved nothing, and only ended up looking like a rather unstable windmill.

I experimented with more steps. It seemed as if the harder I trod the more elevation I achieved. I started to panic. Could I get down? How would I do this if every step taken took me further skywards? Through trial and error I discovered that if I rocked my hips from side to side I would gradually descend. My anxieties abated somewhat, and my delight regarding my newfound ability returned.

Much to my shame, within me my ego gained ascendancy, and I started to desire recognition for my inexplicable skill. I still had no witnesses.

I was, at that point, level with the top of one of Mrs Jones overgrown trees. Mrs Jones lived next door to my abode. She had been on her own since her husband passed away many years ago. Mrs Jones had let her garden go to seed since her spouse's passing. I had the idea, that if I could float my way to the top of Mrs Jones's tree, I could snap off a branch from the top, and thereby prove my ability to traverse through the air.

By dint of many minutes wriggling and stepping I managed to get close enough to the top of the tree to access the uppermost branches. Mrs Jones tree was extremely bushy, and I was not standing on solid ground, so I had nothing with which to provide any leverage. I am not blessed with the greatest strength, my work did not require it, thank goodness, I am not naturally athletic. So it was with some considerable difficulty that I commenced attempting to wrest a branch from the clutches of its origin, but after a lot of twisting and wrenching I was, eventually, successful in my venture.

I pushed myself and my prize away from the uncared for, and uncultivated tree, and wriggled my way gently back to terra firma. Landing was easy, it felt exceptionally good to feel solid concrete beneath my feet again, but this presented me with yet another quandary. Would I be able to walk again as normal? If not how was I to navigate my way through my city. How was I to get home? Would I now have to walk by wiggling my hips as I stepped all the time? I would become nought but a figure of fun, a focus of mass ridicule.

Concentrating hard, I tentatively braved a step. My foot hit solid ground. I was intensely relieved. Slowly but surely I made my way towards my front door. I then started to experience the most intense attack of self-consciousness. Here I was, a well-dressed, well-respected, middle-aged businessman, carrying a rather massive bushy branch of a plain and very ordinary tree. I must have looked, and certainly felt, completely ridiculous. I wondered what my landlady, the ever so fastidious Mrs Brown would say, should she spy me entering her premises carrying a rather large branch. Even worse, what if the wretched Mrs Jones should see me walking off with a large chunk of her tree? What if she should be so offended she brought her argument publicly out onto the street? I sought the sanctuary of my rooms posthaste, lest my reputation be completely ruined.

The normality of my humble abode was such an acute contrast to my preceding experience. I was sweating profusely, my heart was racing, and I was panting heavily. I felt most undignified. Discarding my bowler hat and removing my jacket, waistcoat, and tie, I rushed into my bathroom and stared at my visage in my small shaving mirror. I still looked like me, if but an extremely flustered version. I'm not quite sure what I expected to see. Turning on the cold faucet I splashed my face with water and made a conscious effort to normalise my breathing. After a few minutes of cold water splashing and controlled breathing I rechecked my countenance, and I did look much more composed.

Going into my front room I sat down and just stared at the fireplace. My mind was racing and unfortunately none of it was making any sense to me. I will admit that I started to doubt my sanity. Staring at the branch on the floor, my mind started to clear a little, and I became quite positive that I had actually levitated, that my recent experience was real. However, it occurred to me that, while for me, the branch was indisputable evidence of my experience, any sceptic would scoff at such flimsy proof, saying that the branch could have been easily picked from the lower reaches of the tree. Feeling suddenly dejected, I removed the branch from my sight, and left it discarded on my bedroom floor. I felt exceptionally foolish now.

I turned on my radio and listened to some soothing music, then I decided I would just get on with my usual evening routine. I heated myself a nice steak and kidney pie, which I served with boiled potatoes and some garden peas. Settling down after I ate, with a cup of fresh tea, I felt blissfully normal again. I forgot all about my disturbing experience, finished the Times crossword, and read some of my favourite Conan Doyle. Sherlock Holmes reminded me that even the most inexplicable events do eventually end up having a very rational explanation.

It was only when I retired for the night, at the sight of the discarded branch, I was reminded that, only a matter of a couple of hours ago I was levitating above the streets of Notting Hill. I ignored the branch and tried to push the thought from my mind. I pulled the curtains closed, and retired to my bed, hoping that everything would look different after a good night's sleep.

Unfortunately, a good night's sleep proved hard to come by. I was incredibly restless; my subconscious mind was obviously struggling to process my unbelievably unsettling day. During the night I woke up with the moonlight ebbing gently through the curtains and into my bedroom. The light blue glow clothed the discarded tree branch. I could see the branch starting to snap into the tiniest, small twigs all by itself. I just knew I was not dreaming, I pinched myself and felt the pain. I was absolutely petrified, my skin crawled with goosebumps and the hair on the back of my neck bristled.

The twigs continued to snap, and break and shorten, until they were nought but a brown woody dust pile on the floor. This wooden shrapnel swirled, though there was no breeze, and started to coalesce. A human shape started to form from the wooden dust. My horror turned to awe as the most beautiful female creature I had ever seen was formed from the congealed sludge of my mysteriously disassembled levitational evidence.

This stunningly beautiful creature spoke to me. Her voice sounded like thick syrup and sandpaper; it was hypnotic, and immensely attractive. I was transfixed. I couldn't understand the meaning of her words, it was not a language that was familiar to me. I speak French passably, I can understand a little Spanish, and I studied Latin at school, but these words were like nothing I had ever heard. I would have given anything just to have comprehended even a tiny morsel of what she was saying to me.

I stammered a few words back to her, I tried all my linguistic skills, all the languages available to me, but it was all to no avail, she clearly could understand me no more than I could understand her. She smiled shyly at me, and my heart ached. I fell instantaneously in love. I was under no illusion, I loved her with all of my being, but I knew she could not possibly love me back. My head spun.

This wonderful, mysterious, shy, entity was clearly starting to get restless, she looked around the room, which was obviously strange for her, and I could sense she was starting to become disturbed. I wondered if she was starting to feel trapped in this place so foreign to her. I threw back the curtains, letting the full flow of the moon enter the room, it only served to make her more ethereal and stunning. I opened the window which allowed a fresh spring breeze to access our space. This served to both calm and entrance her, she clambered over the bed, which was next to the window, and the breeze washed over her face, this obviously pleased her immensely, her eyes closed rapturously.

She smiled at me in gratitude. Then she climbed out of the window, and in a flash she was gone. I protested most vehemently; my dwelling is three floors high. Much to my horror I thought she had plummeted to her death. When I looked out of the window, and down to the ground below, there was no sign of her anywhere, she had simply vanished. I strongly suspected that she had disappeared into the nearby trees, though how she could have made such a leap is beyond my imagination. I was however starting to become aware that there were many things that were beyond my extremely limited imagination.

After closing the window and curtains, I lay back down on my bed, I felt most at peace, and I fell immediately into the most delicious, dreamless sleep.

I awoke early in the morning, just before my alarm clock would normally be informing me it was time to arise. I lay, listening to the dawn chorus, and ruminated about my previous day. I absolutely did not know what I was supposed to make of these most peculiar events. I felt different, I knew I was me, and I felt happy enough, but I knew a seismic psychological shift had occurred deep within me, and I was completely dumbfounded as to how to respond.

In somewhat of a daze I arose and performed my usual morning ablutions. I cooked and ate my usual boiled egg and toast, and I sipped thoughtfully through my usual cup of tea.

I went to work as usual and did all the things I usually do. But none of it was the same, unfortunately for me, a 'normal' existence no longer appealed in the slightest. I slid into the most serious malaise. I attempted to maintain my work and to carry on with life as it was, but it was all to no avail. I just could not carry on as normal. I had no appetite, no enthusiasm, for any of it at all.

I started to miss days at work, feigning sickness. After a while I gave up all pretences and just stopped going to work. Being an accountant I had frugally saved a considerable sum and had investments that could be drawn on. Inevitably these funds have dwindled over time, and I am inching ever closer to the point where my current situation will not be financially sustainable.

At this moment in time I know not what the future holds for me, nor how I will both occupy, and end, my days. But I just absolutely cannot go on with life as normal, when I am now acutely aware that it is not.

Sometimes I miss terribly the certainty I used to have about life. I miss the banal normality of everyday life. Everything to me prior to the event was black and white, right, and wrong. Facts and figures were my life and I lived accordingly. The problem I have now is, it appears my previous certainty was built on unsolid foundations, I had a dearth of information about other possibilities; I was, I'm afraid to say, ignorant, my assuredness was false. It appears to me now that the foundations of my previous existence were based on a partial picture, with vital components omitted. I simply cannot go on living a lie.

Today, I admit, I know not what to do, so I simply do nothing. Perhaps I just need to hand over my will to the Gods that be, and just wait and see what occurs?

Thanks to my mam for editing, I owe you a meal.

Printed in Great Britain
by Amazon

84598232R00088